CHRISTMAS COMES TO LIGHTHOUSE POINT

KAY CORRELL

ZURA LU PUBLISHING LLC

TO MY READERS

Dear Readers,

I couldn't resist going back to Lighthouse Point and adding this holiday story. The first six books of the series were originally published in 2017 and 2018. I loved this series and do believe that Tally is my favorite character I've ever written.

So when I decided to go back to one of my series and add a holiday story for 2022, I decided that Lighthouse Point was a great choice. Loved visiting with Tally, Julie, and Susan again. Even Camille!

I hope you enjoy this dip back into the Lighthouse Point world.

TO MY READERS

Kay

ABOUT THIS BOOK

Molly Croft returns to Lighthouse Point to clear out her aunt's cottage. Not that Shannon was really her aunt. She was her mother's best friend until… she wasn't. Molly spent every summer and Christmas on the island until she was twelve. Her mother and Shannon had a huge blowup and they'd never returned to the island and she'd never seen Shannon again.

So why had Shannon left the cottage to her in the will?

Wade couldn't believe Molly was back on Belle Island. She'd been his best friend until she and her mother mysteriously disappeared thirty years ago.

As they renew their friendship, Wade helps her clear out the cottage—who knew Shannon was a hoarder—and they begin to unravel the mystery of what had happened all those years ago. Why Shannon and Molly's mother had never spoken again.

Secrets slowly untangle with life-changing consequences.

Will a wish made at Lighthouse Point thirty years ago finally come true?

A long-awaited addition to the beloved Lighthouse Point series.

This book is dedicated to Christmas past. The lovely Christmas mornings of my childhood spent at my grandparents' house. The big family gatherings. Decorating real trees with old-fashioned lights. Oh, and tinsel. Always lots of tinsels. The joy of seeing beloved ornaments each year. Huge Christmas meals where we'd sit at the table for hours talking and laughing.

We create new memories now, but I'll never forget those Christmases of my youth.

I hope your Christmas memories hold a special place in your heart.

CHAPTER 1

Molly Croft was sure she'd never had a worse task to do in her entire life. A long sigh escaped when she opened yet another crammed closet in her aunt's house.

She'd already boxed up six—count them, six —sets of dinnerware. Enough glasses to allow an army to drink in style *twice*—if not three times. Enough silverware for her aunt to use a unique set each day for over a month.

Stacks of unopened boxes overflowed into the hallway from the two guest bedrooms. So many boxes that she couldn't even get around in the rooms. She'd have to start at the door, open each box, deal with it, and move further in.

Why had her aunt thought she needed to

keep every single thing that ever came through her doors? Molly didn't remember the cottage being like this when she and her mother would come to Lighthouse Point on Belle Island and stay with Aunt Shannon each year. A month each summer and two weeks at Christmas.

Not that Aunt Shannon was really her aunt. She was her mother's best friend. Well, she'd been her mother's best friend from their grade school days until thirty years ago. Shannon and Regina. Inseparable until… they weren't.

Suddenly, Molly couldn't take it anymore. The stale air, the stacks of boxes, the memories that threatened to choke her. She walked over and threw open the French doors to the deck and stepped outside. The welcome sunshine rained down on her, and a fresh, salty breeze blew in from across the waves. She sucked it into her lungs, clearing out the stagnant cottage air. How long had the place been closed up like this?

This musty cottage was nothing like the bright, cheerful one she visited each year as a girl. She was about twelve when her mother and Shannon had a falling out. So the yearly trips abruptly ended. She hadn't been back to the house on Belle Island since the day her mother made her pack up her bag and they'd left. The harsh crunch of the crushed seashell drive as they sped away still echoed in her ears.

Over the years, she'd wondered why Shannon never tried to contact her. After all, the dispute was between her mother and aunt. It hurt her feelings that Shannon had never contacted her. But it wasn't like she was her real aunt. Not family. Though Shannon was the closest thing she had to family, except for her mother. Her mother had been an only child. Her grandparents were gone before Molly was born. Her father died when she was a baby. So Shannon had become Aunt Shannon, and they seemed like family, acted like family. Spent Christmas together each year like family.

Oh, how she'd loved her. Shannon taught her how to put on makeup. Play the piano. She'd been an avid reader and introduced her to so many talented authors. And taught her to bake. She loved spending time in the kitchen with Shannon. Her mother hated cooking and baking and left them alone to their recipes.

But after that one huge argument—which her mother refused to talk about, so she still had no idea what it was about—she never heard from Shannon again. But then, she'd gotten busy herself with school and boys and college and then her career. And she'd never made the effort to come back and see Aunt Shannon either.

Shannon. She should just call her Shannon. No blood relation. But then... why had Shannon left this beach cottage to her? A person she hadn't seen in over thirty years? It made no sense.

Another sigh escaped her, and she wasn't the sighing type. She sank onto a weathered Adirondack chair and kicked off her shoes, leaning back and letting the sun soak through her. It had been cold with the weatherman predicting a storm that was supposed to dump a foot of snow after she left Denver early this morning. The warm weather in Florida was a welcome respite.

When she made plans to come here and clear out the house, she naively thought she'd get it all done in a week. That wasn't going to happen. She brought her computer with her and thought she could get some work done during the day and sort out the house at night.

But at this rate, it was going to take her precisely forever.

Not that she really had any plans. Not even for Christmas coming up in two weeks. Her mother was on a trip out of the country with Craig, her new *serious* boyfriend—so she claimed. Number three just this year. Molly hadn't even told her mom she was coming to Belle Island. They never talked about their summers here. Ever. Shannon's name was never mentioned. She hadn't even gotten up the nerve to tell her mother that she'd inherited the house.

She closed her eyes, remembering her shock when she walked in this afternoon. The boxes. The piles of paperwork everywhere. She'd already planned to stay at the cottage, never dreaming it would be in this kind of shape, so she washed the sheets and made up the bed in Shannon's room. The only room a person could really walk through. Even the kitchen was piled with stacks on the table and barely enough room to get to the fridge, sink, and stove.

Thank goodness someone had come and cleaned out the fridge and threw out food that would spoil. But all the rest had been left up to

her. And the enormity of the task loomed
over her.

What had Shannon said in the letter the
lawyer gave her? She'd left the cottage in *a bit of
a mess*. Right. She'd been surprised that she still
recognized Shannon's swirling penmanship.

My Molly,

*I've missed you so much over the years. You were like
the daughter I never had. I'm sorry that the argument
between your mother and me severed my relationship with
you. I don't blame you for being mad at me.*

*I want you to have the cottage. I hope you come often
and stay and enjoy it. I know I left it in a bit of a mess.
I'm sorry for that. I have all my affairs in order, filed in
boxes, so settling my estate should be an easy matter
for you.*

*Oh, and I left you a letter at the cottage. I'm sure
you'll see it. Please don't hate me. I should have told you
all those years ago. Maybe Regina has by now. I hope so.
Please forgive me.*

Enjoy the cottage and know that I always loved you.

Aunt Shannon

. . .

But she wasn't mad at Shannon. She'd never been mad at her. She just never understood what happened.

But she hadn't found any of the boxes Shannon mentioned, nor the letter, despite working almost non-stop since early afternoon.

She looked down the beach, staring at the lighthouse rising above the water. How she loved walking down to the lighthouse. Swimming in the salty water. Collecting shells. Such great memories.

Until they ended.

She pushed off the chair, took one last look at the soothing waves brushing the shore, and headed back inside. After tugging a ladder over to the bookcase, she climbed up to the top shelf with a box in hand, intent on emptying the shelf. A book of poetry. She paused to read a few of the poems that were bookmarked. Then she grabbed *The History of Lighthouse Point*, complete with photos. Balancing the box on the shelf, she leafed through the book, seeing how the lighthouse had changed over the years. At this rate, it was going to take *longer* than forever to clear out Shannon's house. She stretched her hand over to reach for another book, and the ladder wobbled beneath her. She grabbed the ladder as the box started to fall.

"Hey." A man appeared at the bottom of the ladder, steadying it, then catching the box as it tumbled off the shelf. "You okay?"

"I'm fine." She shakily climbed down, done with heights for a while.

The man turned around from where he was placing the box on the edge of a table. "I saw the door was open and came over to check—" His eyes widened. "Molly?"

She carefully studied the man before her. He was tall and slender with the tan of a local, his hair bleached a light blonde from the sun.

"Yes?"

"It's me. Wade."

She stared at him again. "Wade?" A grin whipped across her lips as she hurried over to hug him.

He wrapped his arms around her and held her for a moment before stepping back. "How many years has it been? But I'd recognize you anywhere. You haven't changed a bit."

She looked up at him—he was so tall now. "Oh, I've changed. And, wow, you've changed."

"You mean from the pudgy twelve-year-old?" He flashed a grin at her.

"No, I just meant... You're... taller." She rushed to cover her embarrassment.

"Nah, that's okay. I kept the pudgy physique until my junior year in high school. Grew eight inches, lost the weight."

"You look great." Really great. She'd never have recognized this version of Wade. Not in a million years. Except for his grin. She recognized that. "What are you doing here?"

"Live next door now. My parents moved to a retirement place up near Orlando. Didn't like the upkeep of the house anymore." He shrugged. "So now it's mine."

"Wow. Nice."

"I heard Shannon gave you her house. I'm sorry about your loss."

"My what? Oh, I am sorry Shannon is gone. I really loved her when I was a kid. But I never saw her again after that summer when she and Mom had that argument and we left. I feel like my loss was back then."

"That's too bad. I kept thinking you'd show

up again some summer. Shannon was so sad after you left. I don't think she ever got over it. She kept working as the head librarian until she retired. She got a bit reclusive after that. She stopped accepting Mom's invitations to come over for dinner. I'd see her out on her porch sometimes and wave or see her in town getting groceries and say a few words, but that was about it. She did get a lot of deliveries though. Kind of a legend in town in that regard."

"No kidding," she said dryly. "The house is wall-to-wall boxes, and it's my job to sort it all out."

Wade swept his glance around the room. "I see that. I had no idea."

"I know. There's not a flat space anywhere that's not covered in paperwork or boxes. And a lot of the boxes aren't even opened."

"Looks like you have your hands full here."

"I know. I hardly know where to start."

"You should start by letting me help you."

"Oh, I couldn't ask that."

"You didn't. I offered. And to say thank you, you'll let me take you to Magic Cafe for dinner tonight."

Her mouth watered at the very thought.

"That doesn't seem like much of a deal for you, but I'd be glad to thank you by going to Magic Cafe tonight." She smiled. "Six? I need to get a shower. I'm all dusty from sorting through stuff."

"Six it is. I'll meet you right back here on the deck. I assume you want to walk the beach way?"

"But of course."

She walked him to the door, and he loped back over to the neighboring cottage, pausing to wave before slipping inside.

Wade Connelly. Wow, had he changed. But then, he hadn't. He was still the easygoing, friendly person she'd spent so many summers roaming the beach with. It would be fun to catch up with him tonight.

CHAPTER 2

Wade stepped up on the porch right at six as Molly closed the French door behind her. He'd put on a collared, short sleeve knit shirt in a bright blue shade that highlighted his sky-blue eyes. He flashed her the smile she remembered so well. The one that came easily and often. "Been a long time since we've gone to Magic Cafe. I used to save up money from my chores to be able to go there with you."

"Shannon used to slip me money so I could go."

"I don't have to do random chores to afford going to Magic Cafe these days."

Neither did she, not that she was flush with funds, but she got by.

"I'm all set." She carried her shoes as they headed to the shoreline. The warm water lapped at her feet and she stopped for a moment, enjoying the sensation. The breeze blowing her hair, the sun on her face. Enjoying being back on Belle Island.

Wade stood by her side, letting her soak it all in. "Lighthouse Point is a pretty special place, isn't it?"

"It is. I can't believe I haven't come back in all these years. What a mistake. And I so wish I would have come to see Shannon. That was an even bigger mistake."

"I'm sure she would have loved to see you."

She turned and looked up at him. "And I don't even know why we left. I have no idea what happened. Mom won't talk about it. She ever has."

"Have you tried asking her recently?"

"I tried… hmm… must have been eight-ish years ago. She refused to talk about it and said to never bring it up again."

"It's too bad Shannon got shut out of your life. She was a great lady. Did a lot for the town."

"I don't suppose she ever talked to you about her fight with Mom?"

"Not a word, sorry."

"I don't think I'll ever find out the truth." She shook her head, clearing her thoughts. "Come on, let's go. I'm starving."

They strolled to Magic Cafe and rinsed the sand off their feet under the spigot at the edge of the beach. They slipped on their shoes and entered the restaurant. Tally walked up to them greeting them with a huge smile. "Wade, I haven't seen you in a month of Sundays. Job been keeping you busy?"

"It has."

Tally turned to her, frowned, then a smile slowly spread over her face and her eyes lit up. "And Molly Croft. Goodness. Look at you. You turned into a beautiful woman." Tally wrapped her arms around her and gave her a quick hug.

"You remember me?"

"Of course. You and Wade. Always together. Every summer and each Christmas. Welcome back." Warmth twinkled in her eyes.

"Thank you. It's still wonderful here. Everything looks the same."

"Not much changes on Belle Island, that's for sure. Is Regina here with you?"

"Ah… no. Just me."

"Oh, that's too bad. I would have loved to see her." Tally grabbed some menus. "You two want inside or outside?"

"Outside," they said in unison and laughed.

Tally led them to a table by the edge of the beach. "We're going to provide one of our spectacular sunsets for you tonight, too. Compliments of the island." She handed them menus. "I'll send Tereza over to get your order."

She settled on her chair with Wade across from her. Contentment spread through her as the familiarity of Magic Cafe, Wade, and the whole island surrounded her.

"You look happy." Wade leaned back in his chair, stretching his long legs out underneath the table. She scooted over to give him more room.

"I am happy." Just then, the white Christmas lights strung along the ceiling and the railings sparkled on. "Oh, that's so…"

"Magical?" He winked. "You know, Magic Cafe and everything."

"And the tree in the corner. So pretty. Look at all those teal ornaments on it."

"Tally goes all out for Christmas decorations."

"If I remember correctly, you do, too."

He shrugged. "Maybe. A little."

"Your mom always said you started to bug her by the first of November to get the decorations up. By the time we got here at Christmas, your parents' house looked like a Christmas factory. Lights. Trees. Garland. Presents. Do you still do all that?"

"I… uh…"

She threw back her head and laughed. "You still do, don't you? I'll have to come over and see it."

"How about you? Is your place all decorated back home?"

She shook her head. "No, I didn't even put up a tree this year since I knew I was coming here to clear out Shannon's cottage. I thought I might put one up when I got back. But now I'm not sure I'll get back before Christmas."

"Are you spending it with your mom?"

"No, she's on a holiday trip with her boyfriend." Were they called boyfriends when a person was in their seventies? Man friend? She chased away her scattered thoughts. "It's just me this Christmas."

"Then you should stay here through the holidays. You don't want to spend it alone. That's not right." He leaned forward, his eyes excited. "We could do all our old favorite things. There's the tree lighting... that's tomorrow, by the way. There's the Christmas sandcastle competition. That's always fun. The sandcastles all have a holiday theme to them. Oh, and Caroling Night in the square."

"How am I going to get Shannon's house cleared out if we do all that?"

"You will, because I'm helping, remember? We'll knock it out in no time."

She looked at him doubtfully. "Maybe."

"So, you'll stay?"

"I'll think about it." And why not? It wasn't like she had plans for Christmas. She was spending it alone. Suddenly, that didn't sound very appealing. It just sounded... lonely.

"You finished thinking about it yet?" He tossed her an imploring, boyish look.

"Yes. I'm done thinking about it. I'll stay. It actually sounds like a wonderful way to spend the holiday."

"Perfect." He leaned back with a self-satisfied grin. "It will be just like old times."

A woman with long black hair and a friendly smile walked up to them. "Wade, hey. Tally said to take extra special care of you two tonight."

"Tereza, this is Molly. She's here, uh, visiting. She used to be a regular on the island. Tereza is one of the best servers here at Magic Cafe."

Tereza laughed. "Don't let Courtney hear you say that." She smiled at Molly. "Nice to meet you."

"Do you still have the fried grouper and hushpuppies? Oh, and the coleslaw. I loved that."

"We do."

"I'll have that and a beer."

"Same for me." Wade handed their menus to Tereza, and she headed to the kitchen. "Courtney is Tally's granddaughter. She's learning the ropes of the restaurant."

"That's so nice to be able to pass the business on to someone in her family."

"And now Tally and her husband actually leave the island and go on trips. Very different than the twenty-four-seven hours she used to work."

Tereza brought their beers, and she took a sip of the ice-cold beverage. "So good."

"It is." He took a sip of his and leaned back. "So, what is it that you do, Molls? You know, when you're not clearing out houses?"

"I do freelance work. Writing mostly. Some corporate newsletters and the like. Some website copy. I also do content management for a few nonprofit companies."

He laughed. "I'm not sure what content management is, but it sounds impressive."

"It's kind of the management of all sorts of content for a company. From their websites, to graphics, to their social media." She took another sip of her drink. "And how about you?"

"I'm a contract programmer. Work for different companies when needed. Have a pretty full list of companies that call me for work now."

"Wow, computers. This from a guy that hated math and science?"

"Well, I found computers and discovered I kind of have a gift for programming. The logic makes sense to me. I really enjoy it. Solving problems. Finding why a program isn't working."

"I'm glad you found something you like doing."

He took a sip of his beer and looked at her over the top of his bottle. "And do you have anyone special in your life?"

"Me? You mean like a boyfriend? No, not now."

"But you did?"

She swallowed, not wanting to relive the last few weeks and some of her motivation for coming to the island now. "I... did. Roger. We dated for five years. A couple of weeks ago, he asked me to dinner at this fancy place. I thought..." The heat of a blush crept over her cheeks. "Well, I thought he was going to ask me to marry him. We'd talked some about marriage and what we wanted from life. We ran in the same circle of friends and had so much in common. We saw each other almost every single day."

"But?"

"But... he asked me there to celebrate his promotion. To vice president. And he was moving to Germany to their corporate offices."

"Did he want you to go with him?"

"He didn't say a word about that. Just that we'd had fun together, and he'd remember me fondly. Fondly. That was his word."

"I'm sorry."

She stared at the beer bottle for a moment, watching a lone water drop slide down the side, then looked at Wade. "I was taken by surprise. But Roger always did want to climb that corporate ladder." She'd been more than surprised. She'd been blindsided. She'd thought that she'd finally found someone who would want to stay in her life.

Not like her mom, who had moved away from Colorado and left her alone to finish college, figure out how to earn enough for school and everything else. It took her six years to get through college with multiple jobs each year and a large school loan, but she'd made it. Now, if she was lucky, her mother came to visit once a year. Maybe.

Then there was Shannon, who never came to find her. Never came to see her. Okay, she could have come back here to see Shannon after she grew up. She knew that. But it still felt like

Shannon had deserted her all those years ago. At least it had to her twelve-year-old self.

"Luckily, you have me to distract you for a few weeks." Wade interrupted her thoughts.

"And I'm glad to have the distraction." She smiled back at him. He was so easy to talk to. A great listener. It took returning to Belle Island to realize how much she missed him.

CHAPTER 3

Tally watched as Wade and Molly left Magic Cafe. They'd thanked her repeatedly for the meal, and Molly proclaimed it was the best meal she'd had since leaving the island years ago. She did so love it when people enjoyed the cafe. The two headed in the direction of downtown. Bet they were going to look at the nice Christmas decorations the town had put up.

Her granddaughter, Courtney, walked up to her. "Busy night tonight. But things are slowing down now. Why don't you go on home? Tereza and I have things covered here."

"You know, I might just do that." She took

off her apron and handed it to Courtney. "Don't forget you're dropping off Bobby tomorrow to have his playdate with Eddie."

"I won't forget. It's all he's been talking about. Guys' day. Pops and Bobby only. No girls allowed." Courtney smiled. "I just hope he's not up at five a.m. wanting to leave."

"We're up that early. Bring him any time."

Tally walked down the steps and turned to look back at the cafe. She loved the place so much. It was like a living, breathing being to her. And now, with Courtney learning the business, she could allow herself to take an early evening like this. So nice.

She strolled along the lamplit streets toward home, enjoying the evening breeze and looking forward to a quiet evening at home with Eddie.

Eddie. How her life had changed since Eddie came back to town. The love she'd had for him all those years ago sprang back to life. Every day with him was a blessing, though he shared her pain of the loss of their son. But out of that loss, they'd gotten to know Courtney and Bobby. She'd gone from no family to a rich, full family life that she was ever grateful for.

Her thoughts popped back to Molly. She

wondered if Molly knew what had happened between Shannon and her mother. The town had been ripe with gossip after the argument with everyone asking where Molly and Regina were. The two of them never missed a Christmas on Belle Island until they'd disappeared. But Shannon had been silent on the subject.

Such a shame to let a rift go on that long. To let it destroy a lifelong friendship. But people were stubborn sometimes. Too stubborn to reach out and try to fix things. Shannon had spoken to her once about the argument, just a few months before she died. She didn't tell Tally all the details, just that she had to right a wrong. Shannon was bedridden by then and wanted Tally to mail a letter for her. She'd sworn her to secrecy though, and Tally always kept her promises.

Still, it was sad that Shannon and Regina never worked things out. And it was sad that Molly hadn't come back for Christmas until now. Sometimes secrets were better hidden in the past. But then... sometimes they weren't. But it wasn't her secret to tell.

Wade led the way to the downtown area of Belle Island. Bright Christmas lights stretched across the street, with wreaths adorning each lamppost. Every store window was decorated for Christmas with ceramic villages, cheerful garlands, and snowflakes. Not that the island would ever see snow.

Molly peeked at each window, exclaiming with excitement at each display. He'd forgotten how even the little things would make her light up with joy. And until today, he hadn't realized how much he'd missed her. Their friendship. Talking to her. Or maybe he'd forced himself not to remember…

She looked at him and smiled. "This is fun, isn't it?"

"It is. Let's head down Oak Street to the gazebo. It's all draped in lights, too. Very festive."

Music spilled out the open door to The Lucky Duck as they walked down the street. "Oh, can we go in for a minute and listen?" Molly slowed down.

"Of course." They walked in and Willie waved to them from the bar, motioning them to take a seat.

They sat at a table, ordered drinks—Wade insisting she try one of Willie's famous basil motonics—and listened to the music. He leaned close to Molly. "The singer is Misty Hartman, a local."

"She has a beautiful voice."

"She does."

Molly looked around the tavern. "This is new since I left."

"Willie Layton owns it. Great guy."

"I guess I was wrong when I said nothing changes here. There are changes. New people. New places."

"But most of the things stay the same." He grinned at her. "And I'm still here."

She reached out and grabbed his hand, squeezing it. "And I'm very glad you are."

Misty sang a sad ballad and then changed to a medley of Christmas songs as they sipped their drinks.

Willie came over during Misty's break. "Good to see you, Wade. Been a while."

"Everyone keeps saying that to me. I guess I should get out more." Wade shook Willie's hand. "And this is Molly. She's cleaning out Shannon's house. Shannon was her…" What was Shannon to Molly? Molly always called her Aunt Shannon, but that was really a nickname.

"Shannon was a friend of my mother's," Molly jumped in. "She left her house to me."

"I'm sorry for your loss," Willie said.

Molly nodded. "Thank you."

"So you staying long?"

"She's agreed to stay through Christmas," Wade said. "Took some arm twisting, but she agreed."

"Nothing like Christmas on Belle Island. I mean, we don't have the snow like up north, but the town does it up in a big way."

"I remember." Molly nodded.

"Well, pop in anytime." Willie headed over to chat with another couple at a nearby table.

"He seems nice."

"He is. That's the reason The Lucky Duck is so successful. He greets everyone. Chats with them. Not to mention he has some of the best burgers around."

She held up her drink. "And his basil

motonic. It's really good."

"See, I told you."

"What else has changed around here?"

"Let's see. There's a new bakery in town. The Sweet Shoppe. Run by Julie, a friend of Tally's. Julie's got some of the best pastries I've ever tried. We should grab breakfast there one day while you're here."

"Sounds good. I can't even cook at Shannon's until I get the kitchen cleared out. I did find the coffee pot though."

"Oh, and Belle Island Inn is now owned by Jamie McFarlane and his mother, Susan. You remember the place. Used to be owned by Jamie's uncle."

"I remember it."

"But some things haven't changed. The lighthouse is still here."

"Do people still go there to throw a shell in the sea and make a wish?"

"Sure do."

"Maybe I should go make a wish that everything will magically be sorted, filed, and dealt with at Shannon's cottage."

He laughed. "Maybe you should."

She stood. "We should probably head back.

We've got a busy day ahead of us tomorrow."

"That we do." He stood and followed her outside. As they strolled down the street, she slipped her hand in his, a comfortable connection to a good friend.

They reached her cottage, and he walked her to the door. She turned to him and smiled, her one dimple crinkling in the moonlight and her brown eyes sparkling. She stood on tiptoe and kissed his cheek. "I had fun tonight. Thank you."

He cleared his throat, the kiss still warm on his cheek. "I did, too. I'm really glad you came back to the island."

"I am, too. I've missed it."

"I'll be over first thing in the morning to help you with everything."

"I should say no, that it's not your problem." She shrugged. "But to tell the truth, I could use the help. It's so overwhelming."

"It's always better to share the load." He reached over and touched her arm. "And I'm glad to help. Really."

"I'll see you in the morning, then." She disappeared inside, flipped on a light, and a gentle glow spilled from the windows.

He turned and jogged over to his place, glancing back for one last look at Molly's cottage. He had such a good time tonight. If he wasn't careful, it was going to hurt just as much this time when Molly left as it had all those years ago.

CHAPTER 4

Tally opened the door at six thirty the next morning and Bobby threw himself into her arms. "Grams, I'm here."

Tally smiled over Bobby's head at Courtney. "Early morning?"

"I sent him back to bed twice, but finally gave up." Courtney shrugged.

Bobby pulled away and raced past her and threw himself into Eddie's arms. "Pops. Pops. I'm here. It's our guy day."

"Sure is." Eddie's eyes twinkled as he grinned at Bobby's enthusiasm.

Bobby stepped back and tugged on Eddie's hand. "Are you ready to go?"

"Where are we going first?"

"I'm starving. Can we go see Miss Julie? Then we're going fishing, right? I wanna catch a big one this time. Enough to feed a zillion people."

"That big, huh?" Eddie laughed. "If you two women will excuse us, it looks like we're heading out."

"And after fishing, we're getting burgers from The Lucky Duck and eating them at the gazebo. Then we're gonna practice making a sand-snowman. Pops and I are entering the sandcastle competition this year. I bet we'll win."

She ruffled Bobby's hair. "I wouldn't be surprised."

"Bye, Mom. See ya tonight. Bye, Grams." Bobby raced to the door.

Eddie gave her a quick kiss on the cheek. "See you tonight if there's anything left of me after our big day." He grinned as he headed out the door.

She and Courtney stood in the doorway, watching them as they climbed into the car. Courtney waved as Bobby stuck his hand out the window, waving vigorously. They headed inside and she picked up the coffee cups left on the table.

Courtney glanced at her watch. "I better get to the cafe."

"Here, I'll walk with you."

"I thought you were taking the morning off to go see Julie and Susan?"

"Not until mid-morning. I'll go help at the cafe until then."

They strolled along the short walk to the cafe, chatting about Christmas gifts for Eddie. Tally knew she spoiled him, and Courtney told her she was overdoing the Christmas gifts. Maybe she was. But it was a grandma's prerogative to spoil their grandchild, right?

"You're going to meet us at the tree tonight for the lighting, aren't you?" Tally asked.

"Of course. Wouldn't miss it for anything. Bobby is so excited." Courtney laughed. "So much excitement for one day."

"I'm glad he's getting to participate in the town's traditions. They make the island a very special place at Christmas."

"There's nowhere I'd rather be this Christmas."

"Is AJ coming home soon?"

"Yes, he should be back in a few days. He's

visiting his grandmother since he'll be here for Christmas. He's sorry he's missing the tree lighting though. I think he wanted to see Bobby's reaction."

"He'll be back by the sandcastle competition, then?"

"Yes. He wouldn't miss it. When he gets back, you and Eddie should go on another trip."

"He has been a wonderful help at the cafe, hasn't he? Really getting the business side of things sorted out. Maybe we will take another trip. But after Christmas."

"Good. I love how you two travel now that AJ and I can run the cafe."

"It is nice. I'm not used to having time away." Tally smiled. "And you look really happy these days. I love that."

Courtney stopped, turned toward her, and gave her a big hug. Then she stepped back, her eyes shining. "I am happy. Happier than I've ever been in my life. I never thought that life could be like this. No longer hiding from Kurt."

"That ex-husband of yours can't hurt you again. He's all safely behind bars."

"I know. And I have a family. A man who

loves me like AJ does. And Bobby is nuts about AJ, too. The two are inseparable."

Tally's heart swelled with the happiness Courtney was feeling. As far as she was concerned, life was just pretty perfect these days. She felt the same way as Courtney. She never knew life could be like this. Wonderful and full of so much joy.

Tally walked into The Sweet Shoppe at ten, as planned. Julie and Susan were already seated at a table and waved to her. She joined them as Julie poured her a cup of coffee from the pot on the table.

"It seems like forever since we've actually found time to get together." Tally sat down next to Susan and reached for the coffee.

"I know. I've been busy with the inn. All the repairs we're doing," Susan said.

"It looks great. All sparkly with its fresh coat of paint." Tally loved that Susan and Jamie no longer struggled to run the inn. It was making them a good living and enough to keep up with repairs. The rooms were full of customers almost every day. They were doing a booming business with weddings there, too.

"Well, we aren't three single women anymore. We have businesses to run and husbands. We are busy." Julie shoved the plate of pastries toward them.

"Wonderful husbands," Susan said as she reached for a croissant with chocolate drizzled over it.

"We're very lucky women." Tally eyed the plate of mouthwatering goodies, wondering which to choose.

Julie laughed. "Go ahead, Tally. Have more than one."

Wavering a bit, she made up her mind and grabbed a pastry. "I'll have the raspberry Danish." She took a bite. "So good."

"Julie is trying to get us fat with all her great baking." Susan laughed.

"Do you have a lot of catering jobs for the holidays?" Tally took a sip of coffee, and as good as the raspberry Danish was, she wondered if she should have followed Susan's lead and had a chocolate-drizzled croissant.

"I do. Pretty well booked up. And get this. Camille Montgomery actually asked if I could cater one of her mama's holiday parties." Julie rolled her eyes.

"She did not." Tally's eyes widened. "After accusing you of stealing the last time you catered their party?"

"You turned her down, right?" Susan asked.

"You bet. I crossed my fingers behind my back and told her I was all booked up. Then I accepted a job that very afternoon for the night Camille wanted me. So it was almost the truth." Julie's laugh rang out. "Does that make me a horrible person?"

"No. It makes you a prudent person. And why would she ever think you'd work with her again?" Tally shook her head.

"I don't know. Maybe everyone is turning her down after they heard what she did?"

"Serves her right." Susan frowned. "She's just not... nice."

"That's an understatement." Julie leaned back in her chair. "Anyway, I hope to never need money so much that I ever take a job from her or her mama."

"Not likely. You do know you married a very rich man," Susan teased.

"I did. But The Sweet Shoppe is all mine. I don't want him bailing me out."

Tally leaned over and covered Julie's hand. "And look how far you've come. From working for me to having your own business. A very successful business."

"I'd never have gotten this far without your help all those years ago."

"You're a very hard worker. That's why you're successful. That, and you're an excellent baker." Tally sat back and took another bite of the Danish, still eyeing the croissant. But really, she couldn't eat both. That would be wrong.

Julie laughed, scooped up the croissant, and dumped it on her plate. "Here, have a bit of both of them. You know you want to."

"I do," she admitted guiltily. "You make the best... well, the best everything." She sat back in her chair, happy and content that they'd made time for each other. Because that's what best friends do.

CHAPTER 5

Molly stood in the kitchen boxing up the cookware. She'd counted twenty different pots. And maybe a dozen frying pans of various sizes. She kept out some cookware and bowls to use while she was here and boxed up the rest. Then she rescued the rolling pin out of a box and kept it too, the wooden handle worn smooth from use.

She planned to donate all the items to the rummage sale at the high school. They held an annual sale to help fund extras not covered by their budget. One year, she remembered, they funded the high school band's trip to march in the Rose Parade. Another year they added more equipment to the grade school playground. This year it was to replace some outdated computers. But since it was this weekend, it didn't give her much time.

Wade called out from the back door she'd left propped open to air out the cottage. "Molls? You here?"

"Come in."

Wade walked into the kitchen with a bag and two cups of coffee. He held them up. "Stopped by The Sweet Shoppe. Grabbed some cinnamon rolls and coffee."

"Oh, thank goodness. I couldn't get the coffeemaker to work this morning." She cleared off a space at the table. Kind of. Enough that they could at least sit and eat.

Wade opened the bag as they sat down, and the delightful aroma of cinnamon and yeast filtered out. Her mouth watered as she reached for a cinnamon roll. "You're the best."

"I thought you might need a bit of fortification for the day ahead." He smiled and attacked his cinnamon roll.

After their breakfast, she stood and stared at the room. "I'm not making much progress, am I?"

"We will. Come on. I brought boxes over,

too." He went out to his truck and returned with a stack of boxes. "One room at a time. We can do this."

They started in the kitchen. He packed up the rest of the cookware while she sorted through the pantry, throwing out expired items. Some light corn syrup from *ten years* ago that had turned dark with age, canned goods that had expired ages ago, and boxes of cereal. So many boxes of cereal. Any food that was still good, she packed up for the food pantry. She kept a few items so she could cook some of her meals, but not much.

Then she found it. Shannon's recipe box with its worn, faded recipe cards. She took it out and leafed through it, then pulled out a card with Shannon's recipe for sugar cookies. She ran her fingers over it with a smile tugging at her lips. How many times had they baked those together, decorating them in bright Christmassy colors and bringing them to Caroling Night at the gazebo? Suddenly, she jumped up and grabbed some of the cookie sheets out of a box to keep them, too. Maybe she'd have time to bake some cookies. She looked around and laughed at herself. Or maybe she should just stick with the task at hand. She set the recipe box aside to pack up with items she wanted to keep. An ever-growing stack.

Wade finished boxing the cookware and looked at the coffeemaker to see if he could fix it for her and discovered the circuit was blown on the outlet. He fixed the circuit and now she could have her morning coffee.

After a few hours, the kitchen started to look cleared out. Wade carried box after box out to his truck. "We should run what we have to the high school and the food pantry. And how about some lunch?"

"That sounds great. I could use a break. Can we go to The Lucky Duck and get those burgers you talked about?"

"Sure can."

They dropped the boxes off, then headed to Oak Street. Her eyes took a moment to adjust to the dim light in the restaurant after the brilliant sunshine outside.

"Hey, welcome back. Grab any table," Willie called from behind the bar.

They headed to a cleared table, and Wade paused to talk to an older man sitting with a young boy. "Eddie, good to see you. And hi, Bobby."

"Hi, Mr. Wade. It's a guys' day for Pops and me. I caught the biggest fish ever, didn't I, Pops?

"Mighty fine catch." Eddie grinned. "Could feed a zillion people."

"See, I told you." Bobby bounced up and down in his seat.

"Molly, this is Eddie and Bobby. Eddie is Tally's husband. Eddie, this is Molly. She's here cleaning out Shannon's house."

"Nice to meet you," Eddie said. "Quite a job cleaning out a house, isn't it?"

"It sure is." She nodded.

"That's why I'm bringing her here for Willie's burgers. Fortification."

"Good choice."

"You and Bobby have fun on your guys' day," she said as they headed to their table. They sat down and she leaned forward. "I didn't know Tally was married. Though I did meet her granddaughter."

"She and Eddie got married just a little while ago. Heard they were together years ago, and he came back and found her."

"Oh, that's sweet. I'm happy for her."

They had their lunch, and she had to agree, it was one of the best burgers she'd ever had. They headed back to the cottage, and she took a deep breath as they headed inside, steadying herself for the task ahead.

They moved into the family room. Wade started boxing up a curio cabinet while she browsed through the bookshelves, pulling out a few books that she wanted to keep. It was hard to give away so many books. Hundreds of books, shelved alphabetically by author. But they did no one any good just sitting here on the shelf. She got to the last bookshelf and found a file stuck at the end of it. She opened it and gasped. "Look at this. She's got every single book listed that she has on these shelves." She ran her finger down the first page of *A* authors.

"You know, I bet if you showed that list to the new librarian, she might want some of them."

"That's a great idea. I'll check with her, then we'll box up the others. Well, except for my stack of books I want to keep." She glanced at the towering stacks of books she'd pulled, not realizing she'd saved so many. "Guess I'm not much better than Shannon when it comes to books."

"You and Shannon always were big readers. I'm not surprised you want to keep so many. I'll box yours up, label them, and we'll put them aside."

She turned to a wooden file cabinet in the corner. Maybe that would have the elusive files Shannon had mentioned or the letter. She opened the drawer and slowly started pulling things out. Knitting patterns, travel brochures, and what looked like the manuals for about every item Shannon had ever bought.

A box was tucked in the back of the drawer, and she pulled it free. The battered top fell off. She looked inside and frowned. It was filled with envelopes addressed to her in Shannon's pretty handwriting. Picking up a stack tied in a faded ribbon, she checked the postmark. It said it was sent years ago, but it was marked return to sender, not at this address. And she recognized that handwriting, too. Her mother's. Envelope after envelope. Same thing.

She opened the first envelope and gasped. A birthday card for her thirteenth birthday with a letter tucked inside. She read the letter full of birthday wishes and chat about Shannon's life. Hot tears began to roll down her cheeks.

Wade came over and knelt beside her. "What's wrong?" He put his hand on her shoulder.

She looked up at him through her tears. "These are letters from Shannon. I never got them. Mom must have intercepted them and sent them back. Why would she do that?"

"I'm not sure."

She looked at the stacks of letters. Years' worth. "She did try to contact me. Wrote to me. All these years." Sadness mixed with anger swirled through her. "I never knew she wrote."

"That must have been really hard on Shannon to get all these sent back."

She swiped at her tears. "Mom had no right to do this."

"Maybe she thought she was protecting you."

"From what? Whatever their fight was about didn't involve me. Shannon must have kept writing, hoping one would get through." She looked up at Wade. "I miss her so much. Being back here makes me realize it. I should have come back to see her. I shouldn't have deserted her."

"You didn't desert her. Your mom took you away and kept her from contacting you."

"But once I was older. I could have come back. Could have visited her. But I never did. I regret that."

"We all make choices that we regret sometimes. We have to learn to live with our choices and make the best of them." He reached down a hand and pulled her to her feet. "I think we've done enough today. How about we get cleaned up and head to the Christmas tree lighting?"

Wade was right. She needed a break. And she was covered in dust from the messy job of sorting through everything. "Good idea."

"Sunset is at about five thirty this time of year and the tree lighting is at seven. I'll pick you up about six thirty and we'll walk?"

"Yes, sounds good."

"What about dinner for you?"

"I'm not very hungry. Still full from lunch."

"I'll see you later, then." He walked to the porch door and turned back to her. "You sure you're okay?"

"I'm fine. Or I will be."

He slipped out the door and she sank back to the floor, grabbing another envelope from the box. She slowly read letter after letter until she glanced at her watch and realized she only had twenty minutes to clean up and get ready. She put the rest of the letters back in the box and hurried off to get cleaned up.

CHAPTER 6

W ade walked back over to Molly's and called from the open door. "You ready?"

"Just give me a couple of minutes."

He walked over and lounged against the deck railing, waiting. A light breeze blew in from the water, and a flock of gulls swooped by overhead. He stood there, remembering how many times he'd done this before. Picked her up to walk to the tree lighting. Though back then it had been Molly, her mother, and Shannon. Just the two of them tonight. Kind of bittersweet.

Molly walked outside, her hair still damp from a shower. "Sorry, I got lost in reading more of Shannon's letters."

"Did she say anything about the argument she had with your mother?"

"Not much. Just that she hoped it wouldn't prevent us from still being close. She said…" Her voice cracked. "She said I was like the daughter she never had. And that she missed me. Why did I stay away? Why?"

He pushed a lock of her hair back from her cheek and wiped away a lone tear. "You were just a young girl when it all happened."

"But later? I should have come back."

"You didn't know she'd sent all those letters. You're going to have to find a way to forgive yourself."

"I don't think I ever will."

"Ah, Molls. We all have to learn to deal with our past. I know you're sorry. Shannon wouldn't want you to feel bad about what happened, either. She loved you."

"She did." She turned and looked out at the water before looking back at him. "Which is why what I did is so much worse."

The pain in her eyes seared his heart. "I'm sorry, Molls."

She drew in a deep breath. "Me, too. But for now, I'm going to put all my regrets aside and just enjoy going to the tree lighting with you again."

He grinned at her. "It's kind of like old times, isn't it?"

"It is. I'm really excited about seeing it again. I haven't ever lived in a place that has a real tree lighting celebration. Not like Belle Island."

"Then we should go. Don't want to miss it." He took her hand in his and led her toward town. Her hand, the connection, it just felt right. He had to remind himself to keep his feelings in check. She was leaving after Christmas. And once again, his friend would be gone.

He glanced down at their intertwined hands. He'd just have to enjoy every moment they had together for the next few weeks. Show her all Belle Island had to offer at Christmas. Then... maybe she'd come back again to visit.

Tally and Eddie stood with Julie, Susan, and their husbands, sipping on hot chocolate. Tally loved the tree lighting night. They even closed the cafe early each year so all her employees could come. She felt it was an important part of the holidays that everyone should have a chance to experience.

Eddie squeezed her hand. "You always did love this night, didn't you?"

"I do."

"I'm glad I get to share it with you again." He kissed her lightly on her cheek.

Courtney came hurrying up to them. "Have you seen Bobby? He asked me if he could hang out with his friends by the gazebo, but when I checked with them, he wasn't there." Her eyes clouded with worry.

Eddie reached out and put his hand on her shoulder. "I'm sure he's just wandering in the crowd."

"But..." Courtney's eyes clouded with concern.

"Sh, no, Kurt is in jail. He can't hurt you. Can't hurt Bobby. He's safe." Tally rested her hand on Courtney's arm. She was glad that Courtney's ex-husband was safe behind bars, but she still was concerned that Bobby was missing. "Let's split up and look for him."

"You mean this guy?" AJ came walking up

to them with Bobby holding his hand and jumping up and down.

"Mom. Mom. Look who came home."

AJ walked over and kissed Courtney. "Told Granice that I couldn't miss the tree lighting and she understood. Ran into Bobby here on the way to the gazebo. Bought him a hot chocolate and a cookie."

"Yes, look. It's chocolate chip. My favorite." Bobby held up a huge cookie.

"You said you were going to go see your friends."

"I started to, but then I saw Miss Mary with Stormy. I had to pet Stormy, didn't I? Then I saw AJ."

Courtney gave Bobby a kiss and held him close.

Bobby squirmed out of her arms. "Aw, Mom. Stop it. You're smothering me."

"Everything okay?" AJ asked.

"Just fine," Courtney said, the color returning to her face. "I just couldn't find him for a few minutes."

AJ draped his arm around Courtney. "Sorry to add to your worry. Should have brought him right over instead of stopping for treats."

"No, that's fine. I'm just a bit overprotective."

"You have every right to be," Tally said. "But you don't have to worry now. Belle Island is safe." Well, safe now that Kurt was behind bars.

The mayor stepped up to the microphone. "Welcome to the annual tree lighting."

A cheer went up from the crowd.

"Are we ready to get this thing started?"

"Yes," Bobby called out.

"Okay then. Ten. Nine."

The countdown began, but this year, instead of watching the tree lights come on, Tally turned to watch Bobby. He called out each number of the countdown, and his eyes grew wide as the lights came on.

"Mom. Look at that. Hey Pops, did you see that? Wow." He tugged on AJ's hand. "Wasn't that cool?"

"Definitely the coolest thing I've seen in a long time," AJ said and ruffled Bobby's hair.

A group of band members from the high school started playing Christmas carols, and the crowd milled around. Wade and Shannon walked by and Tally called out, "Merry Christmas."

"Merry Christmas," they said in unison.

She had a feeling about those two. They'd been so close all those years ago. Best friends. Inseparable when Molly came to town. It looked like their friendship had picked right back up from where it had left off. Maybe now that they were adults… it could become even more.

It was Christmas. Everything was possible at Christmastime.

CHAPTER 7

Molly spent the next few days working her freelance jobs in the mornings— after taking an early beach walk each day—and Wade came over each afternoon to help her sort through the rooms. Each afternoon, they dropped off another load of items for the rummage sale. She found a closetful of nice clothing that she gave to the women's shelter. At least all these things would go to someone who could use them.

They dug through boxes that still had shipping labels on them and had never been opened. A random assortment of different items. A selection of coffee pots, two bread makers, six lamps, three bedspreads... and the list went on and on.

"I guess retail therapy was Shannon's thing," Molly said as they placed the last box into Wade's truck.

"I'm going to go run these over to the school, then how about you come over for dinner tonight? I'll pick up steaks and we'll grill out."

Her stomach growled in response to the offer. "That sounds great. But we could just go out to eat. I hate for you to go to any trouble. You've already done so much."

"No trouble. Come over in about an hour or so?"

"I'll be there." She watched as he pulled away, his tires crunching on the shell drive. She didn't know what she would have done without all his help. They'd knocked out so much of the clutter. She'd found boxes of paperwork that she'd set aside to sort through, but most of the other things were donated and all the clothing was gone. She could actually walk through the rooms now.

She eyed the stacks of boxes of things she'd

decided to keep in the main room and shook her head. Maybe she had hoarder tendencies, just like Shannon. Ignoring the stacks, she wandered back to the room she used to stay in when they visited. It still had her twin bed—no longer smothered in boxes. It was silly, but once they'd cleared it out, she'd washed sheets and made up the bed and moved in here. It felt like *her* room. Her space. The same bedspread was on it, although now a faded teal color, and the yellow flowers had paled to a cream color. She walked over and sank onto it as memories rushed at her. Listening to music in the room and her mother calling out for her to turn the volume down while Shannon insisted it didn't bother her. Curling up in the stuffed chair by the window, reading a book. Waking up to the smell of bread baking in the oven or Shannon's delicious coffee cake. She loved that cake. She made a mental note to look up the recipe in the recipe box. She'd saved a cake pan, hadn't she?

She got off the bed and went to the bookshelves, empty now. But she'd kept a boxful from this room, too. A picture of Mom, Shannon, and her when she was about eight sat in a silver frame on the dresser. She picked it up and stared at it, memories rolling through her mind. Picnics on the beach. Movie night in town. Building sandcastles. But mostly it was the time learning to cook with Shannon.

She left her bedroom and wandered into the kitchen, the old familiar clock still ticking away on the wall—or maybe Shannon had replaced it with one just like the old one. A clock couldn't last over thirty years, could it?

Sunshine filtered through the white curtains in the window over the sink. She walked over and smiled as she looked at the items on the windowsill, still not packed up. A piece of sea glass. A pretty lilac-colored shell. An old bottle in a faded teal color. Shannon was always finding things and displaying them on her windowsill. She said they made her happy. Then she'd find something new, and the display was ever-changing.

She would take these with her, too. To remind her of Shannon's love of the simple things she found. But, for now, they'd stay in the window, making her smile. She debated reading some more of Shannon's letters but just wasn't ready for the emotional tug they brought with every word.

Picking up the recipe box, she leafed through the cards, remembering the strawberry pie, the almond scones, the best sugar cookies ever. She could almost taste them. And Shannon's pie crust. Perfected to an art. She could make a good pie crust herself after Shannon taught her, but Shannon's had some kind of magic. Mouthwatering, flakey crust.

Suddenly, she whirled around and grabbed her purse off the counter. The market. She was going to go to the market and get some baking supplies. She glanced at the clock. She had just enough time to shop and make it back to go over to Wade's. It was probably silly to stock up on baking supplies when she was leaving soon, but she didn't care. She wanted to bake in Shannon's kitchen again while she could.

Molly finished putting the baking items in the pantry and fridge, then headed over to Wade's. She climbed up the stairs to the deck and stood in the doorway. "Wade?"

"Come on in. I'm in the kitchen."

She stepped inside, and Christmas land exploded around her. A large tree stood in the corner, ablaze with lights. Garland hung across the tops of the row of French doors leading out to the deck. Stockings hung from the bookshelf, and cheerful snowmen were scattered on the shelves and end tables. There wasn't a flat surface in the room that wasn't covered with Christmas decor.

She laughed as she walked into the kitchen —also heavily decorated. "I see you haven't lost your love of all things Christmas."

"No, I haven't. My favorite time of the year."

"No kidding," she said dryly, looking at the Santa, Mrs. Claus, and Rudolph on the windowsill and a Rudolph clock on the wall. He'd even draped Christmas lights along the large windows in the room.

He flashed a grin at her. "Some things never change, do they?" He twisted the cap off a beer and handed it to her.

She took a sip. "Doesn't it take you forever to get this all put up?"

"A bit of time, but I enjoy it. What's Christmas without a *tiny bit* of decoration?" He grinned and grabbed a plate with two steaks on it. "Let's head outside. The grill should be ready for these soon."

They sat on a glider, waiting for the grill to get hot. "So, did you read more of Shannon's letters after I left?"

"No, I—" She laughed. "I went to the market. Bought baking supplies. I know, I know. But I was looking at Shannon's recipes and I couldn't help myself."

"You should bake some of her cookies for Caroling Night."

"You know what? I should. That would be so fun. We did that every year." Sadness crept over her. "But it won't be the same without Shannon."

"It won't." He squeezed her hand. "But you'll always have those memories."

"I do want to bake in her kitchen again. It's calling to me."

"Then you should bake to your heart's content. We've gotten most of the house sorted out."

"We have. I still have the storage closet to do. I peeked in it and was surprised, but it's not all crammed with boxes. Just the things that were in it all those years ago. I think I'll work on that tomorrow."

"I've got to go help set up for the rummage sale. I volunteer there most years. I could meet you for caroling later by the gazebo, if you want."

"I'd like that. I haven't gone caroling since we left. It seems like I say that a lot. Things I haven't done since leaving Belle Island. It's like my new mantra."

"You're back now, and I'm just your man to make sure that we do each and every thing thing on your list. We still need a long beach walk and have to go to the lighthouse. Oh, and there's the baking contest. Why don't you enter this year? You can sign up at Caroling Night. That would be fun. Shannon used to win it often. It was nearly always Julie or Shannon."

"I'm not as good a baker as Shannon."

"Oh, come on. It will be fun. Who doesn't love a little friendly competition? You could use one of Shannon's recipes. She'd be so proud of you. I know she would."

She frowned, mulling the idea over. "Maybe I could. If I find the right recipe." The idea of entering baked goods from one of Shannon's recipes appealed to her. Like a last tribute to her. She turned to Wade and nodded. "Yes, that's a great idea. I'm going to do it."

"If you're doing some trial runs, I offer up to be a taste tester for you."

She laughed. "You always did love Shannon's baking."

"I do. And yours. You used to always bake with her. Remember that time you made me that apple pie?"

She rolled her eyes. "I made it all by myself. I think I was about eight then? My first pie. It was... horrible. I can't believe you could choke it down."

"It wasn't so bad."

"Liar."

"Okay, it was awful." He chuckled.

"Thankfully, I got much better at them as the years went on."

"Looks like you're going to be pretty busy while you're here."

And she didn't mind. She loved doing all these lovely traditions. They soothed her soul and made her feel at peace. And oh, how she loved being out of the city, the snow, the smog, and here on Belle Island.

After their dinner, they went back out on the deck and sipped on glasses of wine. The stars twinkled above them. She didn't see skies like this back home in the city. Not unless she drove up into the mountains and went to stay at Sweet River Lodge, her favorite place in Sweet River Falls. She tried to get out there at least once a summer. She took long hikes and enjoyed browsing in the shops in town. Especially Bookish Cafe with its eclectic selection of books and excellent coffee. The quaintness of Sweet River Falls reminded her of Belle Island in a way. Touristy during season, but it still kept its small-town feel.

"Did I lose you, Molls?"

"What? Oh, no. I was just thinking about back in Colorado. I saw they were getting ten inches of snow dumped on them today. I don't miss that." She looked down at her bare feet. She could get used to what passed for winter in Florida.

"Won't see snow here for Christmas."

"But I will see white sand. That's even better. It's such a luxury to just walk outside my door and down to the beach. You know how we got rid of all those vases of shells that Shannon had?"

"Yep."

"Well—" She smiled guiltily. "I confess I'm filling a glass bowl with shells I've found. I swear I'm going to have to find a larger place to live when I get back home. I've put so much stuff aside to bring back with me."

He laughed. "You never could resist picking up shells. Then when you'd pick one up and decide you weren't going to keep it, you'd toss it back into the sea and say 'fly free little one.'"

She grinned again. "I confess. I caught myself doing that this week."

"Old habits are hard to break."

She pushed up off her chair. "I should probably head home. It's getting late."

"Or you could stay for another glass of wine."

"I—" It was tempting, but she really did want to tackle the storage closet tomorrow and see if she could get it all sorted out.

"Come on, Molls. We still have so much catching up to do."

She laughed and sat down. "One more glass." She never could say no to Wade when he flashed his boyish grin at her.

CHAPTER 8

The next morning Molly sat on the floor, going through a box of paperwork. Old bank statements... like twenty years' worth. Each stuffed with copies of checks. Shannon had evidently never heard of online banking to pay anything. She finished with the box, pushed off the floor, and hauled the box to the ever-growing to-be-shredded stack.

Tired of sorting through paperwork—still no letter that Shannon had mentioned—she decided to tackle the storage closet at the end of the hall. A small walk-in closet. It had been full of games, decks of cards, and Christmas decorations.

She walked down the hallway and tugged

open the door, stepping into the past. The same shelves loaded with every board game imaginable. How many hours had they played Monopoly, Scrabble, and Clue, or when she was younger, Chutes and Ladders? She'd learned how to play rummy, canasta, and hearts. Oh, and Rook. How much fun she'd had playing Rook. She ran her hand over the stacks of cards held together—barely—with crumbling rubber bands.

Maybe she'd keep a few of the board games and some of the cards. She shook her head. At this rate, her car would be crammed so full of things she wouldn't be able to see out the back.

She pulled out a box of Christmas decorations, and her breath caught. Their stockings. She picked them up one by one. Shannon. Regina. Molly. Red striped with their names embroidered on them. She held them close to her chest, closing her eyes as Christmas morning memories danced before her. Getting up early and opening presents, then a big Christmas breakfast. Egg casserole, coffee cake, fresh fruit.

Once they quit coming to Belle Island, Christmas morning had never been the same.

Her mother usually took her shopping right before Christmas and just put the bags of clothes under the tree to "open" on Christmas morning. No special book from Shannon. No perfect gift that Shannon always seemed to choose. One year a silver necklace with a moonstone that she still had and loved. Once a delicate wind chime that she'd hung by her window in her room. Every year Shannon gave her a new journal, too. She'd kept up her daily journal writing all these years, though she now bought her own new journal each year. This year's was a teal leather-bound journal with thick cream pages. She hadn't found the perfect one for next year, but she should get one soon. The year was almost over.

She set the stockings on the shelf and dug in the box. Her favorite ornaments were in the same battered shoe box. Bubble lights. She wondered if they still worked or would even be safe anymore. Pulling another box off the shelf, she exclaimed in delight at the wind-up Christmas angel. She twisted the base and set it on the shelf. The angel slowly spun in a lazy circle while *Silent Night* played out in musical notes, now slightly off count.

She turned and pulled another box off the shelf. Shannon had labeled it neatly. Regina's things. She opened it up and pulled out a letter addressed to her mother from Shannon. She frowned. Debating opening it, she finally set it aside. It was addressed to her mother, after all.

A few other things rested in the box. A scarf she recognized as her mother's favorite all those years ago. Then she uncovered a charm bracelet and held it up, fingering the charms. She remembered this. Shannon had a matching one. Shannon and her mom always bought two charms when they found one they liked and sent the matching one to the other person. She fastened it on her wrist and the charms jangled softly.

In the corner of the box, something was wrapped in a yellowed embroidered handkerchief. She slowly unwrapped it. A tarnished silver heart ornament hung from a red velvet ribbon. She turned it over and frowned as she read the engraving.

Merry Christmas, you have my heart. J

Who was J? And why was this in the box that Shannon labeled as her mother's things?

She fingered the ornament, then slipped it in

her pocket. She had so many questions for her mother, and undoubtedly her mother wouldn't answer them. She never did.

Closing the door to the closet, she headed to the kitchen, determined to bake a batch of cookies to bring to Caroling Night.

Tally looked up to see Julie enter the kitchen at Magic Cafe. "Here's the fresh bread you ordered."

"Thanks. Our special this week is fried grouper sandwiches, and we're using up your buns so fast." Tally reached for the tray loaded with fresh-baked buns.

"No problem." Julie leaned against the counter. "Sounds like you've been busy here at the cafe."

"Very. Not that I'm complaining."

"Luckily, you now have Courtney and AJ to help."

"I do." Tally poured a cup of coffee.

Tereza came into the kitchen. "Oh, good. More buns. I swear every single customer is ordering the fried grouper sandwiches this week."

"That's what I was just telling Julie."

"Hey, Tereza." Julie reached out and took the offered coffee. "Tally, you going to Caroling Night tonight?"

"No, I'm working. I want Courtney and AJ to go and take Bobby."

"I bet Bobby will love it."

"He's sure excited about going."

"You should go with them," Tereza insisted. "I can close up the cafe. Most of the island will be caroling, anyway."

"Are you sure?"

"I'm positive. You don't want to miss it. Go."

Tally wavered. It was hard to walk away and leave the cafe in someone else's hands, but Tereza was more than capable. "Okay, I think I'll take you up on your offer. I would like to go."

"Perfect, it's decided." Tereza walked back out into the cafe.

Tally sat on a stool next to Julie. "So, have you decided what you're going to make for the baking contest?"

"Not for certain. It will be strange not to have Shannon entering this year."

Tally nodded. "She always gave you a run for your money. I swear it was like you two traded off first and second place each year."

"Though there was that one year that Camille Montgomery entered. Remember? She got second place and was so ticked off she didn't win."

"I remember. Then later we found out she had some fancy chef from New Orleans make her entry."

"A fact she didn't share with the judges. She acted like she made that cake. And I admit, it was delicious." Julie shook her head. "I couldn't believe Camille could bake like that."

Tally laughed. "And she didn't. But you can always count on Camille for causing some kind of trouble."

"At least she wouldn't have the nerve to enter again." Julie gave a wry smile. "Or at least I don't think she would."

"You never know with Camille."

CHAPTER 9

M olly headed into town that evening. The downtown area was teeming with people waiting for the caroling to start by the gazebo. Townspeople smiled and waved and called out Merry Christmas to each other. A piano had been placed up on the gazebo with a speaker system. That was new since she'd last come to Caroling Night.

She brought the boxes of cookies she'd baked over to the tables at the edge of the park area.

"Thank you." A woman reached for the box. "We love having lots of cookies for Caroling Night. The crowd gets hungry after all the singing."

"They're my aunt's recipe."

The woman looked at her for a moment. "Shannon's?"

She nodded.

"You must be Molly. Heard you were in town. I'm Julie. I own The Sweet Shoppe here on the island."

"Oh, I had some of your cinnamon rolls this week. Wade brought them over."

"Ah, Wade and his sweet tooth. He's a regular." Julie smiled. "I'll miss Shannon at this year's baking contest. We had quite a competition going."

"I—I thought I'd enter this year. Using one of her recipes."

"That's great." Julie handed her a clipboard. "Sign up here. The more the merrier."

She signed up and handed the clipboard back to Julie.

"Looking forward to some friendly competition with you. Will be glad to still have Shannon's recipes in the contest." Julie gave her a friendly grin. "May the best baker win."

"Thank you. I think it sounds like fun."

Julie turned to greet another woman laden with trays of cookies, and Molly wandered around in the crowd. She finally stood at the edge of the gathering, feeling a bit out of place. She'd always had Shannon, her mom, and Wade with her before. A lady went up to the gazebo—oh, that Misty Hartman who'd sang at The Lucky Duck the other night. She sat down and played a few notes, got up, and adjusted a couple of the speakers.

Misty started playing *We Wish You a Merry Christmas*, and the crowd began to join in. Wade slipped up beside her. "Just made it in time, didn't I?"

"Just in time." She smiled up at him, happy to have him here with her. Sharing this night. Candles with holders were passed around, and one by one, neighbors lit each other's candles. Soon, the area glowed with candlelight and Christmas lights.

He reached for her hand, and they stood side by side, singing each holiday song. Just like they had all those years ago. The past and the present swirled around her in a comforting blanket of familiarity.

Tally watched as Bobby carefully held his lit candle, making sure that the wax didn't drip off the holder. He sang the carols with gusto—albeit a bit off-key. No one seemed to mind.

"Grams, I only know the first verse to this one." He tugged on her sleeve.

"That's okay. Just join in on the chorus."

He nodded his head and whispered loudly. "I can do that."

Courtney stood next to AJ, his arm around her. Every time he looked at Courtney, his eyes filled with love. Tally's heart filled with happiness at having her family surrounding her on this special night.

Eddie bumped her gently. "You enjoying yourself?"

She smiled up at him. "I've never had a better time at Caroling Night. And I've been to it every year since I was a small girl."

"I'd forgotten how magical it is here on Belle Island at Christmastime." He leaned over and kissed her gently.

Julie and Reed walked up, along with Susan and Adam. "Found you." Julie leaned close. "Quite the crowd tonight."

"No one wants to miss this."

"I ran into Molly. She signed up for the baking contest. Says she's going to use one of Shannon's recipes."

Tally laughed softly. "Looks like you're going to have some competition after all."

"Bring it." Julie grinned.

Eddie threaded his arm around her and his love wrapped around her, pulling her close, warming her. They sang carol after carol with her friends, with all the townsfolk's voices carrying up to the star-speckled sky above them.

Yes, Eddie was right. There was something magical at Christmastime on the island.

CHAPTER 10

After the caroling and Wade feasting on hot chocolate and cookies—though he said hers were the best—they headed to her car.

"Give me a lift? I walked into town today," Wade asked as they got to her car.

"Sure thing. Climb in." She wasn't quite ready to say good night to him, anyway. She was thoroughly enjoying his company. He helped her feel part of the crowd, part of the town.

All too quickly she was pulling into the drive of the cottage. "Do you want to come in for a bit?" She still wasn't ready to say good night and didn't want to be alone in the cottage.

"Sure, sounds good."

They headed inside and she flipped on the

lamp as they entered. Wade stopped in the middle of the room, turning around slowly. "You know what you're missing?"

"Me? What?" She swept her gaze around the room.

"Christmas, Molls. You've got no Christmas. We can't have you staying here this time of year without Christmas." He put his hands on his hips, looking dismayed.

She laughed. "There's enough Christmas at your house for the both of us."

"No, seriously. You need some Christmas. We'll go get you a tree tomorrow." He dipped his chin in an it's-all-decided nod.

"I'll just have to take it down in a week or so."

"So? You'll get to enjoy it until then. I'll help you put it up and take it down. I promise." He crossed his heart.

"I did find some Christmas decorations in the storage closet today." She wavered.

"Perfect. So tomorrow we'll go to the tree lot and get you one."

"I don't know." Seemed like a lot of work for just a little over a week's enjoyment. She swept her gaze around the room. Though it would look nice all decorated…

"Come on, Molls. You know you want to. This place will look so nice all jazzed up with Christmas decorations." He tossed her an exaggerated, imploring look.

She held out her hands. "I give up. You win. There's no denying Wade Connelly his Christmas decorations."

"I knew you'd see it my way." He flashed her a self-congratulatory grin.

She rolled her eyes at him and led the way into the kitchen, where she poured them each a glass of red wine. She scooped up the ornament she'd found in the storage closet and held it out to Wade. "Look what I found. It was in a box marked Regina's things."

Wade took the ornament, turning it over. "'Merry Christmas. You have my heart, J.' Who do you think it's from? It looks old."

"It does. But I don't have any idea who this J person could be."

"That's kind of strange. Another mystery."

"You mean like the unanswered questions about Shannon and Mom's argument? Or the mystery of where the letter Shannon said she left for me is?"

"Like that."

"I don't know, but I'm not sure I'll ever find out. I've tried talking to Mom, and she's just not very forthcoming."

"So still no sign of the letter, huh?"

"No, not yet. But she did leave a letter addressed to my mom." They walked out to the family room and sat on the sofa. "But, no. I didn't read it. Though I was tempted."

"You going to send it to her?"

"I think I'll give it to her next time I see her. Maybe then she'll actually talk to me." She shrugged. "Or maybe not. Let's change the subject. How was the rummage sale?"

"It was crowded. I think they did a booming business. Your aunt's stuff was very popular."

She sighed as regret crept through her. "I'm glad. And I know I kept so much of her stuff. But when I was baking the cookies, I really wished I'd kept her old yellow mixing bowl. I have such great memories of using it. But I know, I know. I kept other mixing bowls. But I regret giving that one away."

"You've got a lot of good memories attached to Shannon's things, don't you?"

"I do. And to her books. I heard back from the librarian. She seriously wants all the books. She said just to box them all up, then she'll put the ones the library doesn't keep out at the biannual book sale."

"Sounds like we have some more boxing to do."

She looked over at the shelves, so full of books she'd read. Ones Shannon had loved. It was so difficult to part with them. It felt like she was giving away a part of herself. But honestly, she'd already kept three boxes of books. Or maybe four?

"It's hard, isn't it?" Wade asked softly.

She looked up into his bottomless eyes, thinking she could get lost in them. So connected to him. He'd always known what she was thinking. What she was feeling.

"I just..." Her voice cracked. "I just miss Shannon so much. Me being here... and her not being here... it's so hard."

He took her hands in his. "I'm sure it is." He brushed a lock of her hair away from her face.

The unruly piece that always fell forward into her eyes and bugged her.

For a moment, she saw something in his eyes. Something different.

Something...

What was it?

He leaned forward the tiniest bit.

She held her breath, her heart dancing in a staccato rhythm.

Her phone rang, and she pulled back, startled. She snatched the phone off the table and frowned. "It's Mom." She clicked on the phone. "Hi, Mom."

"Molly. Where are you?"

"I... uh..."

"I came by to see you, but you're not home."

"You're in Denver? No, I'm not home."

"Where are you? Will you be home soon? I can wait."

"I thought you were off on a holiday trip with Craig." She glanced at Wade and bit her lip.

"I was. But I cut it short. Honestly, that man didn't want to do anything but golf on the trip."

"But you don't golf."

"Exactly. So I told him I was headed home, but he said he was staying because he was signed up for some silly charity golf tournament. We had a big fight. So I came to Denver. Really, I think I'm over Craig. He wasn't the right man for me."

It sounded like *serious boyfriend* was on his way out... No big surprise there. It was like her mother was on a mission to collect boyfriends and discard them.

"Anyway, when will you be back?"

"Why are you in Denver?" She avoided her mother's question.

"Well, I have no Christmas plans now. I got a room at that charming little hotel near your place. I thought I'd spend it with you, of course."

Of course? Like her mother ever included her in Christmas plans? "Mom, I'm out of town."

"You'll be home before Christmas, won't you?"

"I wasn't planning on it." She grimaced.

"Molly, where are you? Where are you spending Christmas?"

She squirmed on the sofa, then sighed,

knowing there was no way out. "I… um… I'm on Belle Island."

Wade squeezed her hand and sent her an encouraging smile.

"Belle Island. Whatever for?" Her mother's words came out in a gasp.

"I'm at Aunt Shannon's house. She… she gave it to me. In her will."

"Her will? Shannon is dead?" Her mother's voice trembled.

"Yes, a few months ago. I was going to tell you the next time I saw you."

"I didn't know," she said softly.

It surprised Molly to hear so much emotion in her mother's voice. She'd made it clear that Shannon was not a subject to be discussed. She didn't exist.

Her mother cleared her throat. "But why would she leave her house to you?"

"I'm not sure. She said I was like a daughter to her."

"Shannon always did like to interfere in things that weren't her business. And you aren't her daughter. She's not even your real aunt," her mother snapped.

She glanced over at Wade, who sat silently

sipping his wine. "She felt like a real aunt to me. I loved her."

"Well, you should come home to Denver now. We'll have Christmas together."

Being her mother's last choice to spend Christmas with didn't appeal to her one bit, but she was her mother, after all. "No, I'm not coming back to Denver…" She took a deep breath. "But you could come here. Stay at Aunt Shannon's house."

"I could never do that. I told her I'd never enter those doors again."

"Mom, seriously. Your fight with her was years ago. And she's gone now. Anyway, I've decided I'm staying here through the holidays."

"Fine. If that's how you want it to be."

The connection went dead.

She set the phone on the table and turned to Wade. "So, did you hear that?"

"Most of it." Wade nodded with a sympathetic smile. "And you invited her to come and stay here. I did hear her answer to that."

"But her answer was a big fat no, wasn't it?" She shook her head. "But I see no reason why I shouldn't stay here on the island and enjoy Christmas. I've signed up for the baking contest.

And we're going to decorate the cottage tomorrow. Right? Besides, I still have boxes of paperwork to sort through. And I haven't found the letter. I'm not leaving before I find it." And now, after being too busy to spend Christmas with her for so many years, her mother wanted to spend Christmas together. But only on her terms. Not at Shannon's cottage.

"Hey, you don't have to convince me. I want you to stay." His eyes shone with sincerity. "I haven't enjoyed Christmas this much since you left."

She looked directly at him. "You know what? Me neither."

But the moment had passed. The moment she almost... *almost*... thought he was going to kiss her.

CHAPTER 11

Molly tossed and turned in bed that night, waking up countless times. One o'clock. Two ten. Three twenty. Her conversation with her mother played over and over in her mind.

She was certain there was pain in her mother's voice when she told her about Shannon's death. Even after her mother had ignored Shannon for all these years. But then, they'd been as close as sisters before the fight.

But her mother had hung up on her. Just click. Then nothing. Who does that to family? And it annoyed her that it hurt her feelings. It wasn't like she and her mother were close. They hadn't spent the holidays together in years. Why did she let her mother upset her like this?

And she hadn't had a chance to ask about J, not that it would have been a good time to bring it up when her mother was so annoyed that she was here on Belle Island.

She flopped over in the bed and punched the pillows, wondering why she'd chosen this twin bed instead of the nice big queen bed in Shannon's room. Moonlight streamed through the windows. Images of sitting by the window and reading danced in her head. Memories of Shannon popping her head in and asking if she wanted to come bake. By five a.m. she gave up and climbed out of bed. She grabbed her robe, slipping it over her pajamas, and headed to the kitchen.

After starting the coffee, she took out the recipe box and sat at the kitchen table. As the enticing aroma swirled around her, she paged through the well-worn cards and pulled out a selection. When the gurgling of the coffee signaled the brewing was finished, she poured herself a cup and headed to the pantry.

By seven thirty, baked goods covered the

counters and table. A pie. Cookies. Shannon's beloved coffee cake. A loaf of bread sat rising near the oven. The delicious aroma of cinnamon, yeast, and baked apples wafted through the kitchen, so familiar and yet so melancholic in a way.

She stood in the kitchen all alone and turned slowly around, missing Shannon with every fiber of her being. With two quick steps, she reached the counter, snatched up her phone, and called Wade.

"Morning." His sleepy voice drifted through the phone. "When I said we'd find you a Christmas tree in the morning, I didn't mean this early."

She laughed. "You better come over here for breakfast. I couldn't sleep so I got up to bake. There's enough food here to feed half the town. Come sample them and help me choose what to make for the baking contest."

"Really?" His voice perked up. "Be there in five."

"Give me twenty. I'm still in my jammies."

"Twenty it is."

She hurried to her room to get dressed,

ridiculously happy he was coming over to have breakfast with her. She paused in front of the mirror as she brushed her hair, half expecting to see the young girl she used to be, not the mature woman she was now. Her eyes sparkled with eagerness at Wade's visit. And why was that? It must just be that she'd been lonely in the kitchen and would welcome the company. That was all it was.

Wade shook his head and stretched, trying to chase away the last remnants of sleep. He rarely slept in this late, but he'd tossed and turned all night. Too many thoughts running through his mind. So many memories of times long ago mixed in with Molly's visit now and how much he was enjoying himself.

He pushed off the bed and headed to get dressed, his mouth watering in anticipation of breakfast. If Molly could bake on her own as well as she used to with Shannon—and her cookies yesterday at Caroling Night were delicious—he was in for a sensory delight.

He shaved, then pulled on shorts and a t-shirt, delighted the weather was still so unseasonably warm. As far as he was concerned, it could stay like this all winter. Not that their winters were bad. They'd have a few lows in the thirties or forties. Maybe a four- or five-day streak of cold weather. But then warm weather would always pop up again.

He'd spent two years in the Midwest after college. The cold, gray, ever-snowing days of winter had finally driven him to head back home to Belle Island. He'd moved home in the fall, just in time to miss one of the hardest winters the Midwest had ever seen.

He'd found a nice little apartment near the beach where he lived until his parents gave him the house and moved to their retirement place. The house had originally been built by his grandfather, and his father was thrilled to have the cottage stay in the family, so it had worked out for everyone.

He headed to the kitchen and poured a cup of coffee from the pot that was set to go off at six thirty each morning like magic. Whoever came up with the idea of automatic coffee makers was a genius. He headed out to the porch, glancing at the time. He still had five minutes to kill.

Gulls called overhead and a lone blue heron stalked along the water's edge. He loved mornings like this. Staring out at the water, he thought back on this week. All the time he'd spent with Molly.

Last night was nice. He'd felt such a connection to her. Kind of like old times… and yet not. Not the best friend feelings like he'd had back then. It was something more.

When did that happen?

He'd been almost ready to kiss her last night but wavered in his decision. But then Regina called, and the moment was lost.

Besides, Molly had just been jilted by her long-term boyfriend. Someone she thought she'd marry. And really, were any of these feelings real? Was he just getting caught up in their easy friendship of before? Was that all this was?

Now was not a good time to try and start something up with her. So many reasons to just let things be. He could rattle off all the logical reasons to remain just friends.

Besides, she was just here for another week or so. Then she'd be gone.

Though he knew, even as just a friend, she'd leave a large hole in his heart. Just like the last time.

CHAPTER 12

"Come in," Molly called out in answer to Wade's knock at the open French door to the deck.

He appeared in the kitchen carrying a mug emblazoned with *make a wish at Lighthouse Point* and a faded imprint of a shell on it. After glancing around at the counters covered with baked goods, he turned to her. "Oh wow, Molls. You've outdone yourself. Look at all of this."

"I know." She laughed self-consciously. "I went a bit overboard. But you need to try everything. I can't decide what I should make for the contest."

"I'm your man. Load me up." He grabbed a plate off the counter.

She filled it with coffee cake, cookies, and a slice of pie. They sat at the kitchen table and he tasted each. Then tasted them again. He leaned back in his chair. "Seriously, Molls, you don't want me to choose. I choose them all."

"That's no help." She shook her head in exasperation. "I have to decide on something."

"I swear you'd win with any of these. They're great." He reached for another cookie.

"I just want to do Shannon proud."

"She would be proud. Proud you're carrying on her tradition."

"I do feel closer to her when I'm in her kitchen, though it was kind of lonely baking here all alone. It was always the two of us. Music blaring from her radio." The radio that was still sitting on the counter and surprisingly still worked. She hadn't been able to give that away either. If she kept much more, she'd have to rent a trailer to haul everything back to Denver. And there was the problem that her apartment didn't really have room for everything she'd saved of Shannon's.

"You should keep trying out recipes and I'll keep tasting them," he teased.

"There are so many good ones in the recipe

box. I remember making so many of them. It will be hard to choose."

"I'm sure whichever one you choose will be great." He drained the last of his coffee. "So, you ready to go get that tree?"

She gathered up the dishes and set them in the sink, looking at the mess in the kitchen. She'd clean that all up later. "We need to wait just a little bit. That bread is ready to pop into the oven."

"Oh, fresh-baked bread. I'm so willing to wait for that."

"I'll put it in the oven, then maybe we can sort out the ornaments and get everything ready to decorate."

"Let me help you clean up the kitchen first."

"You don't have to do that."

"But I want to help." He got up and grabbed a towel from the counter. "Wash or dry?"

"I'll wash, you dry." She filled the sink with hot, soapy water and took the first baking sheet from him.

Soon they had the kitchen all back in order as the yeasty aroma of baking bread filled the kitchen.

"Let's go look for the decorations." She carefully hung the cross-stitched towel to dry. Shannon had added that design and one summer taught her to cross-stitch. With a sigh, she knew she was going to keep the towel, too.

They headed to the storage closet, and she switched on the light, pointing to the far corner. "I found some decorations back there, but haven't looked through everything."

They opened boxes, checked for Christmas decorations, and piled them in a stack outside the closet. She tugged at another box, frowning slightly as she moved it more into the light. Did it have her name on the lid?

It did. Molly.

She opened it and peeked inside. It was filled with wrapped items. She pulled one out. The tag on it said *To Molly* and the year that they'd left Belle Island.

She pulled out another one. To Molly. The next year.

She slowly unwrapped the first one and gasped. Wade turned around to look at her. "You okay?"

"Look…" She held out the leather-bound book. "A journal. Just like she gave me each year. The box is full of them. Do you think she bought one each year for me?"

"Looks like it." He glanced into the box full of wrapped journals.

She clasped the journal tightly, blinking back tears. "I still write in a new journal each year. I'm going to use up all of these."

"I think you should."

She opened the journal to the first page and saw Shannon's familiar handwriting.

My dear Molly, write down your dreams, your thoughts, your troubles. Much love, Shannon.

A lone tear trailed down her cheek. Wade took a quick step and gathered her into his arms. She let the tears fall until there were none left. Still, she stayed in the warmth of his arms, feeling his heartbeat and hearing his low, murmured words of comfort.

Finally, she pulled back. "I'm sorry. I seem to be an emotional mess back here at the cottage."

"No need to apologize. I know it's hard."

He brushed away a tear on her cheek and stared into her eyes. Her breath caught as she looked back at him, trying not to stare at his lips…

The alarm on her phone went off, and she jumped back. "Oh, the bread is done. Let's haul the decorations to the family room and I'll go rescue the bread."

She picked up the box of wrapped journals and hurried out of the room. Once again, her phone had either saved her or ruined the moment. She wasn't sure which.

The smell of evergreens wrapped around Molly as they walked through the tree lot, reminding her of being back home in Colorado. She'd heard on the news that they had twelve inches of snow back home, but here on Belle Island, it was a glorious seventy-nine degrees and sunny.

They wandered through the lot. By mid-afternoon, after Wade inspected every single tree on the Christmas tree lot—seriously, every single one—she paused in front of a perfectly fine tree. "I think this one looks good." She pointed to it.

"No, see… it's dropping too many needles." He shook his head.

"This one?" She pointed to a nearby tree.

"That's a balsam. It will smell good."

"So we'll take this one?" She eyed him. She swore this was the hundredth tree they'd looked at.

"That one over there is a Douglas fir. See how full it is? She's a beaut." He pointed across the walkway.

"So that one?"

He pointed to yet another tree. "That one is a Fraser fir. See how pretty her needles are? And they last a long time."

She didn't mention she didn't need it to last very long, nor did she know that Christmas trees were shes.

"Which one do you want, Molls?"

"You pick." They mostly looked the same to her. This was a side of him she'd never seen. Angsting over picking a Christmas tree. His tree and Shannon's had always already been up when she and her mother arrived on the island. Though Shannon always waited to decorate the tree until after they arrived.

He finally decided on the Douglas fir and they hauled it to his car and tied it to the roof. Then they walked around Oak Street, popping into various shops and picking up more decorations. Wade insisted on new Christmas lights since Shannon's were so old and he didn't trust the wiring. Then he bought some more clear white ones he proclaimed he was putting up on her deck. A lot of effort for such a short time. And although she wouldn't admit it to him, she was kind of excited about getting it all up.

Christmas music spilled out from the open doors on Oak Street. Shoppers filled the stores, calling out greetings to each other of Merry Christmas or Happy Holidays. She couldn't remember having this much fun at the holidays since—well, since she'd left the island. They wandered into a few more stores until she finally insisted they'd shopped enough.

They piled the bags into the back seat, then swung by the market to pick up ham and Swiss cheese to make sandwiches on her bread, and a few other items she needed for some of the recipes she wanted to try.

"I want to make gingerbread cookies. And I remembered a secret ingredient that Shannon put in her sugar cookies. I want to make another batch of them with that included."

Wade's eyes grew wide. "I'm all in on that.

Anything you want to bake, I'll suffer through being your taster." He flashed her a grin as they loaded the groceries into the car.

They got back to the cottage, dragged in all of their purchases, and set the Christmas tree up in the corner. Wade adjusted it. Then adjusted it again.

"I think it looks just fine," she insisted.

"You don't think it leans just the tiniest bit to the left?"

She stared at it. "Ah, no. I think it's straight."

He backed away, eyeing the tree. "I guess so." Then he spun the tree around, looking for the best side to face forward. Then he straightened it again.

Who knew it took this much effort to put up a tree?

She made them sandwiches and sweet tea, and they went outside to sit. It was wonderful to get off her feet for a bit. She'd been standing since early morning.

"I think we found you the perfect tree," Wade said as he lounged in his chair, balancing his plate piled high with two sandwiches on his lap.

"Well, I'm sure you didn't miss looking at even one tree on the lot." She laughed.

"Picking a Christmas tree is serious business. You need to consider so many things."

"So I gathered." She took a sip of the tea and the ice rattled in the glass. "We always had an artificial tree after we left the island."

He put his hand to his heart in mock horror. "Oh, say it isn't so. That's not a Christmas tree... that's a travesty."

"Then I won't tell you I have a small artificial tree in my apartment that I put up each year, either."

"Ah, Molls. Where did we go wrong in your upbringing?" He shook his head, then his mouth eased into a grin.

She sat back and basked in the easy manner of teasing and talking they'd fallen into this week. Wade was so easy to be around. Fun. A bit overzealous on all things Christmas— especially the trees—but a really great guy.

"You're staring at me, Molls."

"I am not."

"You are."

"I just—" She shrugged. "I'm just having a good time this week.

"I am, too," he said seriously and reached over and took her hand. "Don't stay away so long next time."

Next time. Would she ever come back? Once the cottage was sold, she'd have no need to come back. Would she?

CHAPTER 13

After they ate, Wade got up. "I'm going to hang the lights out here while it's still light enough out to see what I'm doing."

"I'll do these dishes while you do that."

It didn't take him long to finish the lights. He plugged them in to make sure they worked, then headed back inside. He'd done a good job of it if he did say so himself. Perfectly draped at precise intervals. No doubt Molly would roll her eyes at him. But there were certain ways that Christmas decorations needed to be done. Evenly spaced intervals on draped lights and garland were one of his firm rules.

He headed back inside and hung garland—evenly spaced, of course—along the tops of the bookshelves. The scent of fresh evergreen filled the room.

Molly came out of the kitchen with a plate full of cookies. "Just in case you need fortification for the tree decorating."

"Don't mind if I do." He swiped a cookie. "Now first we do the lights, then the ornaments."

"Yes, sir. You're the decorating expert." She opened the boxes scattered around them, and he couldn't help but notice the excitement lighting up her eyes. No matter how much she protested, he knew she was really happy about decorating the cottage.

He strung the lights on the tree, slowly spiraling from top to bottom. Another rule. Molly started taking the ornaments out, one by one. "Oh, look at this one. I remember it. It looks just like the lighthouse here on Belle Island."

He smiled at her delight. "I remember that one. Didn't Shannon give it to you?"

"She did." Molly held up a single shell with a loop of fishing line. "And remember this? You made this for me."

He laughed. "I remember. I must have been

about seven? I had my grandfather help make that tiny hole in it, then he taught me how to tie a knot in the line to make the loop. Which then led to a two-hour lesson on tying fishing line knots."

She stood up and hung the two ornaments on the tree before returning to the boxes. "And this one." She held up a picture of the two of them—they must have been about five—framed in a popsicle frame.

"We were cute kids." He grinned.

She looked at it and smiled. "We were, weren't we?"

And they had both changed over the years, but he was thankful their friendship hadn't. At least not since she'd come back to the island. "Hey, Molls, come over by the tree. Let's get a selfie." Might as well have another pic of them. Just to commemorate the occasion was all.

Molly jumped up and stood beside him while he extended his arm and took a photo with his phone. Then another one for good measure.

Molly headed back to the boxes, pulling out ornament after ornament. She entertained him with stories of when many of them had been purchased or who they were given to. Seemed like Shannon had given at least half of them to Molly. When the tree was finally covered in ornaments, she handed him an angel. "Can you reach to put this on top?"

He stood and reached as far as he could, placing the angel on the top of the tree.

"Do you think it would be wrong if I made us some hot chocolate? I know it's not exactly cold weather here…" Molly turned to him.

"I think it sounds like a great idea."

"Okay, but don't turn the lights on until I get back." She disappeared into the kitchen, and Christmas music filtered out from the radio she switched on. After a while, she came back with two steaming cups of cocoa.

She sat on the sofa, and he leaned down to plug in the lights. "Ready?" He glanced at her.

"Yes." She nodded enthusiastically.

He plugged in the lights, and Molly clapped her hands. "Oh, Wade. It's wonderful."

He stood back and had to admit, they'd done a pretty good job. He walked over and sank onto the sofa beside her, reaching for his mug of cocoa. "I haven't had hot chocolate since I was a kid."

"Remember Shannon would make it for us?" She looked at him over the rim of her mug.

"Yes, and put fresh whipped cream on top."

"I didn't think to buy cream."

"This is good without it." It was actually perfect. Everything was. Just sitting here with Molly in the light of the Christmas tree.

They sat like that, with the music drifting around them. Molly rested her head on his shoulder. Before long, he realized she was sound asleep. Not surprising since she said she hadn't gotten much sleep last night. He slowly lowered her to rest on the sofa and covered her with a blanket. She sighed in her sleep and cuddled in the blanket.

He stood there watching her for a moment, a small smile on her lips as she slept. Good. Maybe he'd given her a day to remember. Maybe enough so that she'd come back to visit soon.

Reluctantly, he let himself out, closing the door behind him. Not exactly how he'd hoped the night would end, but they still had time. Not enough time, as far as he was concerned, but it was still a fair bit of time.

CHAPTER 14

M olly spent the next few days trying out recipe after recipe. Wade obligingly tasted every single thing she made.

"You're going to make me put on weight." He patted his stomach. "I actually went for a run this morning, trying to combat the calories I've been consuming."

"These are Shannon's sugar cookies with her secret ingredient." She held out a plate of freshly baked cookies.

"So... what is the secret?" he asked.

"Can't tell you. It's a secret." She grinned as he took a cookie, then snatched another one.

"These are calorie-free, right?" He grinned at her.

"Of course..." She turned away and whispered, "Not."

"Okay, I don't know what her secret is, but these are the best sugar cookies I've ever eaten."

"I thought of making her molasses cookies. I called them gravy cookies when I was little because her icing on them looked like white gravy to me. But I finally decided on these." She grabbed a tray from the counter. "Gingerbread trees. See, you make star-shaped gingerbread cookies in four sizes—each one a bit smaller than the last—and stack them with icing dripping down between them. And I added a tiny star on top."

"Those look amazing, Molls. I remember Shannon making those."

"Luckily, I didn't give away her set of star cookie cutters." She glanced over at the very large and ever-growing stack of items she was keeping.

He took one of the gingerbread trees and broke off a piece. She looked at him expectantly.

"I think we have a winner here." He nodded vigorously. "These are so good. Even the icing on them is spectacular."

She blushed at his enthusiastic endorsement. "Perfect. Then this is what I'll make."

"So for sure, this is what you're making?" He cocked his head to the side, eyeing her doubtfully.

"Well, pretty sure." She shrugged. "I think."

"You know, you'll need to finally make your decision and bake it. The contest is the day after tomorrow."

"I know. It just seems like such an important decision. I really would love to win."

"Who knew you were this competitive?" He smiled.

"I'm not really. Or not usually. But… I just would love to win the contest one more time with one of Shannon's recipes. Kind of a final tribute to her and prove to her how important she was to me, even if she's gone now."

"I'll tell you any of these will give Julie a run for her money."

"You really think so?"

"I really think so."

"And I have to bake extras, too, right?"

"Right. For people to buy. Then all the proceeds go to help fund the library."

"Looks like I'll have a busy day tomorrow."

"Want some help?" he offered.

"Surely you need to work. I've been keeping you so busy with helping me."

"Nope, I'm fine. It's kind of slow this time of year."

"Okay, if you promise not to eat them all up as we make them." She laughed.

"I swear. Cross my heart." He ran his hand across his heart and grinned at her. "Only some of them."

Tally sat at Magic Cafe, sipping coffee with Julie and Susan. "So, Julie, what did you decide to make for the baking contest?"

"I've decided to make cinnamon scones with maple glaze. A new recipe for me, but I think it's really good."

"That sounds delicious," Susan said. "Be sure to make lots of extras, because I bet everyone will want to buy some."

Julie laughed. "Yes, I'll make lots of extras. It will help the library and I'll put the cinnamon scones on The Sweet Shoppe's menu through the holidays."

"You'll probably win. It's almost always you or Shannon. And... well, Shannon is gone. May she rest in peace." Susan poured herself another cup of coffee.

"But her niece, Molly, is entering this year. Using Shannon's recipes. I bet she'll be some stiff competition." Julie shrugged. "Not that I mind the competition."

"It always raises good funds for the library each year. That's the important thing." Tally waved for Courtney to come over to the table.

"Good morning," Courtney said as she walked up.

"Courtney, could you bring us each a slice of that key lime pie we just got in?"

"Oh, cheating on me, are you?" Julie's eyebrows rose, but her lips curled into a smile.

"There's this young lady, Sarah Townsend— new in town—who is starting up her own business. I wanted to help her out. So I ordered a half dozen key lime pies from her for today's special dessert."

"Ah, am I getting some more competition?" Julie asked.

"Maybe, some. I think she's just into desserts that people can order for special occasions and parties. I thought if I offered the pie here and told people about her, it will help her get started. Have a stack of her business cards to hand out."

"You are always helping people," Susan said.

"Like how she helped me when I first came to the island. But actually having Sarah starting her business is kind of nice. I've had to turn away a few jobs like that. I'm getting so busy. If she's good, maybe I could refer to her when I get overflow clients."

"I'm sure she'd appreciate that." Tally was glad that Julie was supportive of this new young woman's business.

Courtney returned with the pie, and they all took a bite. "This is really good," Julie said. "I'd have no problems referring to her if all her baking is like this. Besides, key lime pie is a pain to make. Squeezing all those key limes." Julie laughed. "She could take over all that part of the business."

"I wonder if she's entered the baking contest," Susan said as she took another bite. "This is really wonderful."

"Ouch, you wound me." Julie grinned.

"So it looks like you'll have lots of competition this year. Jay Turner, Lillian Charm's cook at Charming Inn, entered this year. And since they opened it up to anyone in the county, not just Belle Island residents, I heard that Evelyn Carlson from the Sea Glass Cafe over in Moonbeam is entering." Tally eyed Julie.

"The more the merrier. Besides, with more entries, we'll also have more sales for the library," Julie said good-naturedly.

Tally knew Julie loved to win, but she had such a big heart that she didn't mind the competition. She really just wanted the contest and sale to be successful. Tally wouldn't be surprised if Julie won again, even with all the competition this year. She was a talented baker and everything she baked was delicious.

Susan set down her fork and leaned back in her chair. "But at least you won't have to worry about Camille Montgomery. I heard she's been unofficially banned since she cheated."

"Hopefully, she won't even show up this year. Last year she came by my entry and sniffed her nose in disdain." Julie shrugged. "Then she went over to Shannon and made a remark that Shannon had made a strange choice for her entry."

"Does Camille ever make kind remarks to anyone?" Susan's eyebrows rose.

"Probably not." Julie laughed. "But I'd just as soon she stay away this year."

"Don't count on it. Camille seems to show up just like a bad penny." Tally shook her head.

"Or a hurricane," Susan said, and they all laughed.

Tally took a sip of her coffee, wondering what she'd do without her two best friends. They filled her life with sunshine and love. Always there for each other. Always understanding, ever supportive.

She looked over at Courtney chatting with Tereza and hoped her granddaughter could find that friendship with Tereza. There was just something about having best friends. Even better if they'd been best friends for years.

"You're smiling. What are you thinking about?" Susan asked.

"To us." Tally raised her coffee mug.

Julie smiled. "We are quite the best set of friends ever, aren't we?"

"We are," Susan agreed.

They clinked mugs. "To us," they said in unison.

CHAPTER 15

Molly couldn't sleep—it was getting to be a habit—so she got up early the next morning and made multiple batches of the cookie dough and put them in the fridge to chill. Shannon always said that made it easier to roll out and improved the flavor. After grabbing a second cup of coffee, she wandered back into the family room and sat on the sofa. She was certain she'd made the right decision to make the gingerbread trees for the contest.

Well, *pretty* certain.

She stared at the cleared-off bookshelves, the books finally boxed up and delivered to the library. They stood there looking lonely and empty, begging for books. This was all so much harder than she thought it would be. So many memories of times with Shannon. The laughter. The—

She set her coffee cup down with a clatter. Of course! She jumped up and hurried to her room, shoving her clothes to one side of the closet. There, in the back of the closet, she pressed on a wooden panel and it popped open. Their secret spot. Shannon would leave her notes and presents in there. Sometimes there would be one when she showed up for a visit. Sometimes it would appear in the middle of the visit. She never knew.

Holding her breath, she reached inside the opening and smiled. She pulled out an envelope and a wrapped present. Of course. She should have thought of this as soon as she got here. Slowly, she pried open the envelope and unfolded the letter. Moving over to the window for better light, she began to read it.

My dearest Molly,

Of course you found this. I couldn't resist leaving you one last letter in our secret place.

I have something I can no longer keep a secret. It has

rested heavy on my heart for years. I'm hoping Regina has told you by now, but I feel you have the right to know, even though it isn't my secret to tell. I kept my promise not to say a word until my dying day, which is why you're getting this letter after I'm gone.

Your father was not killed when you were a baby like Regina told you. His name is James Jones. Jimmy. A boy from our high school days back in Hays, Kansas. I have no idea what happened to him. Jones. A hard name to track down.

Regina and Jimmy dated our senior year. And, well, no one knew about you. Regina and I left town when she found out she was with child. I've been unable to locate him even though I've tried. I contacted a few leads, but none of them panned out.

I'm not sure if you'll be able to find him either. He's long moved away from Hays. All I know is his birthday is in December and he was interested in engineering. I know, not much. Right? He was going to stay and work a few years before trying to go to college. I have no idea if he ever found a way to go to college.

I hope you already knew all this and maybe you've even met him. I'm sorry I couldn't persuade Regina to search for him and tell him about you. For your sake, I tried, but you see where that got me. Regina left and took you with her.

I've missed you every day since you've left and I pray you've had a wonderful life. Just know that I've always loved you.

    Always,
    Aunt Shannon

She stared at the page she was holding, her hands shaking. Her father was the mysterious J of the ornament. And he hadn't died when she was a baby. He might even be alive. How could her mother keep this from her? Anger raged through her, a fire so intense she had to force herself to breathe deeply and count to ten.

She paced the floor, all the questions running through her mind. Why would her mother keep this a secret all this time? Her father had every right to know about her. Or had her mother told him, and he rejected her? But then, no. Because her mother would have told Shannon that.

She sank onto the bed, still clutching the letter.

So now she finally knew what the fight had been about. About her. About her father. About telling her the truth. The truth both her father and she deserved to know.

Wade cleaned up the kitchen from his early morning bowl of cereal—not nearly as nice as sampling Molly's baking—then grabbed another cup of coffee. He turned at the sound of a knock at the back door. He opened it to find Molly standing there, her cheeks flushed, a piece of paper in her hands. Her brows were drawn and a firm frown etched across her face.

"Come in." He tugged on her hand. "What's wrong?"

"This." She waved the paper. "This is what's wrong." Her eyes flashed with anger and she clenched her teeth.

"Come on, Molls. Tell me what's wrong."

"It's the letter from Aunt Shannon. And she told me what she and Mom fought about."

He pulled her farther inside and shut the door behind her. "Come sit at the table and tell me everything."

She perched on the edge of a chair, drumming her fingers on the worn tabletop. He poured her a cup of coffee, sat down, and pushed the coffee across the table toward her. "What does the letter say?"

"Shannon told me who my father really is. Not some guy that died when I was a baby. It was the J person. The guy from the ornament. James Jones. Shannon called him Jimmy. A boy they went to school with."

His mouth dropped open in surprise. "Really?"

"Yes really. And they fought because Shannon wanted Mom to tell me about him, and try to find this Jimmy and tell him."

This was not something he ever would have imagined the fight to be about. He thought maybe they'd fought over some guy—but not like this. Not about hiding Molly's father. "I'm sorry. This must be quite a shock to you."

Molly's hands shook as she picked up the mug and took a sip of coffee. "I can't believe Mom would keep this a secret. And lie to me all these years."

"Are you going to call her?"

"I am. But… I need some time to process all this first. I'm so angry. So furious." She set the coffee cup down with a clatter, spilling some as the cup settled. "And I don't know if she'll admit the truth after all this time, either."

"Surely she will when you confront her with Shannon's letter?"

"I don't know. She might deny it. She obviously didn't care that she hid the truth from both me and my father for my whole life."

"Are you going to try to find him?" He eyed her.

"I am. But Shannon had little to go on. Evidently, she'd been trying to find him the last year or so but didn't have any luck." Molly's eyes clouded with pain. "I just… want a chance to know him."

It tore at his heart to see the pain on her face. "There's a guy I know. Investigator type. I could see what he says. See what it would cost to hire him."

"Would you? I don't even know where to start, since he has such a common name."

"I'll talk to him today." He reached over and covered her hand. "I'll help you any way I can."

"I don't know what I would have done these last days without you." She leaned forward. "You have been there for me every step of the way. From clearing the house, to encouraging me with the baking contest, to being here for me now."

"There's no place I'd rather be." The raw honesty of his words startled him. There wasn't anywhere he'd rather be. He wanted to be right here. With Molly.

"You've been a big help. Really." She stood. "I should go begin my baking. Baking always makes me feel better. I'm going to put all this aside for today and tomorrow. Give myself time to process it. Then I'm going to call my mother."

He rose. "I'll come with you. I did offer to help."

"You sure? You don't have to."

"I want to." And he did want to. He wanted to spend every second he could with her. Before she disappeared from his life again.

CHAPTER 16

She and Wade walked back to her cottage. She was grateful he wanted to be here with her today. She could use the distraction from the thoughts racing through her mind. Use his support. She wanted to throw herself into baking. Anything to keep her mind off her anger at her mother.

"Okay, what can I do?" Wade asked.

"Pull the first bowl of dough from the fridge. We're going to roll out the dough, then start cutting out the different sized stars."

Wade turned on the radio and tuned it to a station playing Christmas songs. The morning sped by in a blur of carefully rolling out the dough and cutting the stars, baking the cookies, and setting them to cool.

Wade handed her whatever she asked for, washed bowls and cookie sheets, and entertained her with stories of people on the island. The smell of ginger, cinnamon, and molasses filled the kitchen. After just about all the flat surfaces in the kitchen were covered with cookies, they sat at the table and she began stacking the stars into trees and decorating them.

Wade held up a tree he made. "I think I better let you do this part." The poor tree listed to one side, and the icing sat on it in blobs.

"You did that just so you could eat it," she teased him.

"Busted." He took a bite. "These are so good. I bet you win."

"Ah, my biggest supporter."

He patted his stomach. "I am going to be the biggest if you don't quit feeding me like this."

By afternoon, they had all the cookies boxed up to take to the contest and sale tomorrow. Wade helped her clean up the mess, then she sank onto a chair, exhausted. More from the news of the morning than the actual baking.

Wade sat down across from her, a sympathetic smile on his lips. "Long day, huh?"

"Very."

"How about you let me take you to dinner?"

"I don't think I'm up for people tonight." If they ran into even one person who asked her about her mother, she'd scream.

"Then I'm going to cook for you."

"You don't have to do that."

"I want to," he insisted.

"You've already done so much."

"So that's a yes, right? I'll see you at five at my place. Guaranteed not to have any people. Well, I'll be there." His eyes sparkled as he stood.

She smiled. "Yes, that's a yes."

"Perfect."

She stared after him as he disappeared out the door, then sat at the table, staring at the boxes and boxes of cookies on the counter. Two hours until five. Anger at her mother that she'd kept carefully tucked away while they made the cookies bubbled to the surface. The last thing she wanted to do was sit here and let her anger take over. She jumped up from the table and grabbed a sack of flour. There was still time to bake a pie. She'd surprise Wade with one for their dinner tonight.

Wade couldn't compete with Molly's talent in the kitchen, but he could cook a decent meal. His mother had taught him to cook, insisting he'd starve to death if he didn't learn how. And he did get tired of eating out, so the lessons had served him well.

He ran to the market for ingredients and grabbed a bouquet of flowers on the way out. He came home and put chicken in the oven. A rosemary chicken recipe that was easy and delicious. He threw in potatoes to bake, then dug through the freezer and found some green beans. He'd cook those and toss in some almonds. That would do for a passable meal.

He arranged the flowers in a yellow vase his mother had left him. She'd actually left like a dozen vases. What did one do with that many vases? Though he was grateful she'd left them now. He placed the flowers on the table and went ahead and set the table, grabbing some fabric napkins and placemats from the back of the pantry, also something his mother had left. There, that looked nice.

Wandering around his cottage, he picked up a random coffee cup and a plate still sitting on the coffee table where he'd eaten his dinner in front of the TV last night. He straightened a stack of boat magazines and folded the afghan his mother had made him—one of many—and placed it on the back of the sofa.

He looked down at his shirt, dusted with flour and a splatter of grease, and headed to change. After he changed, he paced the kitchen floor, anxious for the clock to finally creep around the circle and hit five o'clock.

He opened the fridge and stared inside. Should he make something else? Was this enough? A knock at the back door drew his attention, and he closed the fridge. Finally. Five o'clock.

He tugged opened the door and Molly stood holding a pie. "I... I just couldn't stop." She shrugged as she ducked inside. "Pecan. If I remember right, you love pecan pie."

"I sure do." He took the pie from her and set it on the counter.

"Yum, smells wonderful. Is that rosemary?"

"It is." It pleased him that she thought the dinner smelled good. He wanted to impress her. Which was… silly, wasn't it? Why did he need to impress her? She knew him so well. The real him.

"Oh, and the flowers. Those are pretty."

Once again, he was pleased that she'd noticed and said something. "Thought they might brighten up the dinner table." But honestly, he'd bought them to please her. She loved yellow flowers.

They stood there for a few moments and silence loomed between them. He cleared his throat. "Ah, would you like some wine? I have a chilled pinot grigio or red wine. Or beer?"

"The white wine sounds good."

He poured them both a glass, then they went into the family room and sat on the sofa. The silence fell around them again. Why? It didn't use to be like this. They'd talk continually from the moment she arrived on the island until the minute she left. But they were young then. Just kids, really. It had seemed easy and natural then.

He struggled to make conversation. "So, are you all ready for the big competition tomorrow?"

"I am. Well, I think I am. I'm still second-guessing my decision. Shannon also had the delicious pecan sugar cookie recipe."

"She did. And she used it to win last year." He grinned.

"Ah, a piece of information I didn't know."

"Your gingerbread cookie trees turned out great. I'm sure they'll be a big hit at the sale, too."

"I hope so." She turned and looked at him for a moment, her face a mask of seriousness. "Wade? Can I ask you a question?"

"Of course."

"Do you… Do you like living here on the island? Living alone?"

"I do like living here on Belle Island. The city was just too much for me. Noisy. Rushed."

"And living alone? Do you like it?"

"I've grown used to it." That was almost the

same thing, right? "Did you and Roger live together?"

"No, we each had our own place."

Why did he like that answer so much? "And you? Do you like living alone?"

"I guess so. I haven't lived with anyone since my college days. It gets lonely sometimes. Especially since… since Roger broke up with me."

"I'm sure that was a big adjustment."

"We used to do things together a couple times during the week, and most weekends. Then all of a sudden I had all these nights free." She shrugged. "It's not like I can't keep myself busy. There's always extra work. And I love to read. And bake. But it's quiet now. I thought I'd hate the quiet… but I don't. I find that I'm enjoying it."

"I love the quiet here, too. Sitting out at night and watching the sunset. Staring at the waves. Watching the sandpipers race along the water's edge." He laughed. "Maybe I'm just a loner type."

"I have to admit, as I get older, I feel less of the urge to go out and do something. Staying in with a good book is a perfect night for me." She looked at him closely. "And have you had any serious girlfriends?"

"A few. One I thought might be... well, the one. You know? But she had other plans. Dumped me for another guy from where we worked."

"Bet that was awkward."

"It was. But then, I moved back here to the island and never regretted that decision." The timer went off and he jumped up. "Let me just check on things. I'll be back in a minute."

When he returned, Molly was standing in front of the bookcase, a picture frame in her hand. "This is us," she said as she turned around.

"It is." He nodded.

"You have a picture of us up in your house?"

"Of course. You were a big part of my life. You meant a lot to me." She meant a lot to him still.

She set the photo back on the shelf and laughed. "I think we need a new photo. I had pigtails and skinned knees in that one."

He laughed. "Okay, let's get a new photo." He tugged her hand and led her outside. He stretched out his arm and took a series of photos of them with the beach in the background and a brilliant display of the approaching sunset.

He scrolled through the photos on his phone, showing them to her.

"Those are great. Make sure you text them to me," she said as she headed inside.

Oh, he'd send them to her. And he planned on printing one and framing it, too. A nice keepsake of this time together.

They had dinner and Molly insisted the meal was delicious. He basked in her praise. They finished off the meal with her pecan pie, which he insisted was the best part of the meal.

After cleaning up the kitchen, they went and sat on the sofa again in the low glow of the Christmas tree lights.

"You want to watch a movie?" he asked.

"*It's a Wonderful Life*?" She looked at him.

He grinned. "But of course. That's your favorite Christmas movie, isn't it?"

"It is. We used to watch it every year, remember?"

"I do." He got up, found the movie, put the disc in the player, and hit play.

He sat back down and she leaned against him, reciting some lines right before the actors said them. He watched her face light up at her favorite parts of the movie. She enchanted him when she mouthed the lines of the actors. And clapped her hands in delight when Jimmy Stewart and Donna Reed sang *Buffalo Gals* and harmonized—off-key—on the final lyrics.

With her close to his side, his heart filled with happiness. Then the nagging idea started to nibble at his mind. A kiss. Just one simple kiss. Which was ridiculous, because she was leaving. Because she was getting over a broken heart. But, oh, how he wanted to kiss her. But he wasn't sure how she'd react. If she'd want him to kiss her.

He should ask her. That's what he'd do. If he could screw up his courage.

He looked down at her, and she'd grown still. Her eyes were closed, and she was fast asleep.

Well, this time he couldn't just get up and leave like the last time she'd fallen asleep on the couch. That was at *her* house. This was *his* house. He pulled her closer, tucking her up against his side, and tugged his mother's afghan around them. Molly snuggled close and sighed.

The opportunity for a kiss was gone, but it wasn't such a bad way to spend an evening. He thought about waking her up, but instead, he continued to watch the movie, content to just sit and have her near.

CHAPTER 17

Molly awoke with a start, confused by her surroundings until she realized she was at Wade's. Light streamed in from the windows. What time was it? She glanced at her watch. Seven. She'd spent the entire night here. She sat up and tugged off the afghan covering her.

Wade came walking out of the kitchen with two steaming mugs of coffee in his hands. "Morning, sleepyhead. Thought you might want this."

She reached for the cup gratefully. "Thank you." She took a sip. "I guess I fell asleep in the middle of the movie, huh?"

"Luckily, it ended the way it always has." He grinned at her.

She ran her fingers through her hair, trying to shove it back into place. "Sorry about that. I should have gone home. Why didn't you wake me?"

"You were sleeping so peacefully. I couldn't bear to. So I just let you sleep."

She fingered the afghan resting beside her. "I guess I was tired."

"And today is your big day."

"It is. I'm kind of nervous. I keep telling myself it doesn't matter if I win, but then… I'd love to do Shannon proud and win it for her. But either way, I should go get ready."

"I'm still picking you up at nine to haul all the boxes to the park, right? Each entrant has their own table to put their baked goods out. A high school kid is assigned to each table to collect the money, so you don't have to worry about that."

Good thing she had Wade. She hadn't known any of those details. She stood, trying to smooth the wrinkles from her slept-in clothing. She took one last sip of her coffee. "I should run."

"I should send you home with another cup of coffee."

"I'll take you up on that." She handed him her cup and their fingers brushed.

He looked at her quickly, then took the cup and disappeared into the kitchen. She stared down at her hand, half expecting her fingers to look burned from the heat of his touch. She shook her head. Silly thoughts. She needed to wake up.

She carefully took the cup he brought her, making sure not to touch this time. He walked her to the door.

"Okay, I'll see you in a bit," she said as she slipped outside, then crossed the distance to Shannon's cottage. He was still standing outside on his deck, so she waved to him as she went inside.

She went into the kitchen and looked at the stacks of boxes, then looked at the clock. Time enough to sit for a moment and calm her nerves. She was just nervous about the contest, that was all. But she stared at the mug in her hand and her fingers wrapped around it. She could still feel his brief touch.

And last night, sitting and watching the

movie. It had been so familiar, like they'd done so many times before when they were kids. And yet, it had felt different.

Everything seemed to feel the same yet different these days. The past swirling around with the present. Old memories mixing with new ones.

And there was the startling fact that her father hadn't died when she was a baby. She was calling her mother and confronting her with that fact. But first, she needed to get through the baking contest.

Tally hurried into the park and waved to Julie, who was setting up her table. Julie had covered the table with a bright red Christmas tablecloth and was busy setting out the cinnamon scones. On a single white plate in the middle of the table sat the four scones that the judges would have. Julie had placed some silver ornaments around the plate.

The judges this year were Harry Moorehouse, who owned Island Property Management, Dorothy, who worked at Belle

Island Inn, the new minister from the methodist church, and the mayor.

"It looks good, Julie. Very festive."

"Thanks. I figured a little bit of extra decoration wouldn't hurt."

Tally nodded across the way. "There's Sarah Townsend. I should probably go over and say hi. She doesn't know many people in town yet."

"Sure, go scope out the competition. And once the sale starts, will you go buy one from each entrant? I want to taste my competition."

"Will do."

Tally went over and chatted with Sarah, trying to make her feel welcome and included. Sarah had made little key lime tarts. Then she walked over and said hi to Jay, the chef from Charming Inn before stopping to talk to Evelyn from over in Moonbeam. She looked down at the box she was carrying with a sample from each table. Julie had a lot of competition this year.

She crossed over to Molly's table. Molly nervously placed her gingerbread trees as Wade held an open box for her.

"These are darling, Molly."

"Thank you." She ran her hands down her

hips. "I'm a bit nervous. I've never entered a competition like this."

"Molls' cookies are delicious. Trust me," Wade said with an easy smile. "I sampled them."

"A lot of them." Molly shook her head, but a smile played at her lips. "I'm lucky to have any left to bring here for the bake sale."

"Hey, it's not my fault. They were so good that I just had to keep trying them." He winked and Molly laughed.

There was something going on there. An electricity between them that was clear to Tally. Though they both looked oblivious to it.

"Well, I'll take one." She bought one and placed it in the box she was carrying. "Good luck."

"Thank you," Molly said as she adjusted the center plate with four gingerbread trees once again.

After buying a sample from each entrant, about twenty in all, she headed over to Julie.

"So, are you going to try all of these?"

Julie peered into the box. "Which one is Sarah's? The key lime tart?"

She nodded.

Julie took a bite. "That's great. And who made these cute gingerbread trees?"

"Those are Molly's."

Julie broke off a tiny piece and tasted it. "Oh, that is good. Really good."

A mocking voice came from behind her. "What are these?"

Tally turned at the sound of the familiar voice. "Hello, Camille. Good to see you. They're cinnamon scones with maple icing. Delicious."

Camille turned up her nose. "Not very traditionally Christmassy, are they?"

Julie balled her fist and pasted on a smile. "Thought I'd try something different this year. A wonderful pastry for Christmas morning."

"I guess." Camille frowned. "I wonder what Mama is planning to have for Christmas morning. I should ask her what cook plans to make."

"You should," Julie agreed noncommittally. Tally could see her struggling to keep from rolling her eyes.

"I saw that woman—Shannon's niece is it—made a more traditional entry. Gingerbread trees. I doubt they're as good as Shannon's baking though. Didn't Shannon win almost every year?" Camille looked innocently at Julie.

Tally knew Camille was well aware that Julie won almost as often as Shannon.

"Sure did." Julie turned her back on Camille to grab another box of scones and did roll her eyes this time.

"Julie wins often, too. And her scones this year are delicious." Tally defended her friend.

"Oh, probably." Camille flipped her hair back over her shoulder with a flounce. "Well, best of luck to you." There was not an ounce of sincerity in her words.

"Thanks, Camille." Julie turned back around and smiled broadly.

Camille turned and walked away.

"She's always such a pleasure to talk to." Julie rolled her eyes yet again.

"Don't let her get to you."

"Oh, I won't. She's just… something, isn't she?"

"That she is," Tally agreed. Camille always spoke before thinking, making clueless, if not heartless, remarks. "But that's her problem, not ours. We only have to worry about who's winning this year's contest."

"I'm in for some stiff competition, judging by the samples I tried."

"But it's all for a good cause." Tally laced her arm around Julie's waist.

"It is. And honestly, as much as I love to win, I wouldn't mind if Molly won this year. Shannon would surely be smiling down from heaven if that happened."

"That she would."

CHAPTER 18

Molly smiled and thanked the friendly woman who bought two of her gingerbread cookie trees, then stepped back and whispered to Wade. "I didn't know people decorated their tables. Look at Julie's. It looks so pretty."

Wade swept his glance around the park. "There are just as many undecorated tables as decorated."

"But the tablecloth and ornaments are a nice touch." She eyed the decorated tables with a twinge of jealousy. Why hadn't she thought to do that?

"Sorry, I didn't think to mention to you that sometimes people decorate their tables. But now you'll know if you come back and compete again next year."

She stared at him. She couldn't compete next year. The cottage would be sold and she wouldn't have her kitchen. She probably wouldn't even be here for Christmas next year. A pang flitted through her, knowing all that she'd miss. She'd have no reason to be here on Belle Island next year.

Before she could tell Wade that she wouldn't be back, he leaned close. "Here come the judges. That's the mayor." He nodded toward a man with a wide smile, carrying a clipboard.

"Molly Croft, is it?" the mayor asked as he approached her table. "So, I hear you're Shannon's niece. You've got high standards to live up to."

She smiled weakly. "I do. Shannon was a wonderful baker."

"So, these are gingerbread cookie trees?" the woman asked.

"Yes, they are." She nodded.

"They look delightful. What a clever idea to make trees by stacking the star cookies."

"Molly, this is Dorothy, the mayor, Harry, and Pastor Cliff."

"Nice to meet all of you." She nodded at them and handed each one a cookie tree.

They each took a bite and scribbled notes on their clipboards. She scanned their expressions, trying to tell if they liked them or not, but she couldn't get even a hint. She looked up quickly at Wade and he smiled encouragingly at her.

"Thank you so much," the mayor said as he finished making his notes. "And we appreciate your participation in this year's contest and sale."

The judges turned to leave and she let out a long breath. "That was nerve-racking. I couldn't tell anything, could you? Do you think they liked them?"

"They'd be crazy not to." Wade hip bumped her lightly and grinned.

Before long, she sold out of her cookies. "I should have made more." She eyed the empty trays.

"You made tons. They were just a big hit."

An announcement came over the speaker system that the winner would be announced in ten minutes. They cleared up the table and crossed over to the gazebo. She stood nervously by Wade's side, waiting for the mayor to make the announcement.

He took her hand in his and squeezed it. She welcomed the comfort and support. She shouldn't be hoping so much for this win. It was just a baking contest. But oh, did she want to win. So badly. For Shannon, more so than herself. So one of her recipes would live again. A silly thought, but it was how she felt.

Wade had bought samples from some of the other entrants, and each one had been delicious. Especially Julie's cinnamon scones. The maple icing drizzled on them was the perfect touch. She didn't think she'd win against those scones. But at least she wanted to place.

The mayor stepped up to the edge of the gazebo. "Welcome, welcome. Another great year for our baking contest. We broke our record for funds for the library. Thank you to all of you for your support. And a big thank you to the bakers that generously donated their baked goods."

The crowd clapped in appreciation.

She shifted from foot to foot. Could he not just get on to announcing the winners?

"So, without any further ado, in third place…"

She held her breath.

"Is Evelyn from Moonbeam's own Sea Glass Cafe for her delicious eggnog cookies."

She took her hand from Wade's and clapped politely, then slipped it back in his grasp. He gave her a reassuring smile. Evelyn went up and got her award, then the mayor stood by the microphone again.

"And second place goes to a first-timer at our contest."

She held her breath.

"Sarah Townsend, for her wonderful key lime tarts."

She looked up at Wade, her hope falling. She'd at least hoped to place in the contest. But now there was only one more spot and, to be honest, Julie should probably take that place. Her scones were simply delicious.

"And now for what you've all been waiting for, our winner."

The crowd grew quiet. She held her breath and shifted from foot to foot.

"Our first-place winner is—" He paused and threw his arms wide. "We have a tie. Next year we're going to make sure we have an odd number of judges." He laughed. "The winners are… Julie from The Sweet Shoppe and Molly Croft, our own Shannon's niece. We're going to have to print another award certificate. Congratulations to both of you."

Wade whooped, scooped her up, and swung her around, her feet flying. The crowd broke into applause. Her heart soared. She'd done it. Shannon would have loved to see this. If only she could have been here. That would have made the moment perfect.

He set her down, and she hugged him again, beaming.

"Go on, go get your award." He nudged her.

She walked up to the gazebo, feeling a wide goofy grin on her face, her heart soaring with happiness, proud of her success.

Julie met her at the gazebo and they both held one side of the award certificate as the crowd cheered. Julie leaned close. "Congratulations. Your cookie trees were delicious."

"So were your scones."

Julie looked up at the sky. "I swear I feel Shannon looking down at us, smiling."

She glanced up at the brilliant blue sky dotted with white, fluffy clouds. "I do, too," she whispered. "I do, too."

CHAPTER 19

Molly and Wade went back to her cottage. She still felt like she was floating on air. It was silly to be this ecstatic over winning a contest, but it felt like Shannon was right here with her. She could almost see her smile, hear her congratulations, feel her hug.

They walked into the cottage and she spun around, her arms wide. "I'm just so happy right now."

He laughed. "I can see that."

"I'm going to pour us a celebratory drink." She headed to the kitchen and poured them each a glass of wine, then returned to the family room. She handed a glass to Wade, then raised hers. "To Shannon's recipe."

"To the woman who baked it and her success." His mouth curved into an infectious smile as they clinked glasses.

Her heart full, she wandered over by the window, looking out at the view. "You know, I really love this cottage. It's going to be so hard to sell it. I'd forgotten how special it is."

He walked up beside her and put an arm around her shoulders. "It is very special."

She leaned against him as bittersweet memories clashed with her happiness of today's victory and her feeling of belonging here. As silly as it seemed, she *did* feel like she belonged here. That she was part of the island. She had to remind herself she was only here to clear out the cottage. To sell it. She let out a long sigh. "I'm so glad I came back here to the island. That I had one last visit to the cottage. That you were here, and we got to know each other again."

He squeezed his arm around her shoulders. "I'm glad you came back here too, Molls. Very glad." He paused, looked down at her face for a moment, then continued, "And it doesn't have to be your last visit to the island, does it?" His eyes flickered with an undisguised hopefulness.

"I... I don't know."

His brow furrowed, and he searched her face, looking for... for what? She blinked under his unwavering gaze.

"I've been wanting to ask you a question for a while now." His blue eyes pierced the distance between them, holding her locked in their depths.

"Ask away." She nodded, mesmerized by those eyes that darkened into a simmering sapphire blue.

He took a deep breath, then blurted out, "Molls, I'd... I'd really like to kiss you."

"You would?" She sucked in a deep breath, surprised...

And yet was she?

He took her wine and placed their glasses on the table, taking her hands in his. "Very much so. I've wanted to since the moment I saw you almost falling off that ladder."

"Not one of my finer moments." Her thoughts were racing, bouncing through her mind.

"So, what do you think? A kiss?" His eyes flashed like summer lightning.

Her heart pounded with answering thunder.

With no hesitation, she knew what her answer would be. "I think that would be nice. Very nice."

"If you could put your phone down so it won't ring, or the alarm won't go off." He laughed. "No interruptions this time. I feel like I've waited my whole life for this moment."

She nodded and set her phone down, turning off the ringer for good measure. There was no way she wanted an interruption this time. Her heart pounded as she turned back to him, seeing his eyes blazing with desire.

He stepped close and pushed that unruly lock of her hair away from her eyes. She swallowed and tried to breathe, her pulse racing.

He leaned close and she could feel his warm breath on her face. She closed her eyes, impatient for the kiss. Finally.

The doorbell rang, followed by a crisp knock, and Wade swore under his breath as he pulled back slightly.

Her eyes flew open.

"Ignore it." He stared into her eyes, holding her gaze.

She shook her head. "I... I can't. I don't know who it could be, though."

He stepped back with a long sigh. "See if you can ditch them and we'll start back up where we left off." He touched her face gently, trailing his finger across her cheek.

She tried to pull herself together as she walked over to the door, noticing her flushed cheeks as she passed the mirror. With a long glance back at Wade, she tugged it open, then gasped. "Mom, what are you doing here?"

"You invited me to come, remember?" Her mother walked past her and into the cottage, looking around the room and dropping her purse on a chair. "It looks... so much the same." Her voice quavered the tiniest bit.

"It does." That was all she could think to answer. The last time they spoke, her mother had hung up on her. But now, here she was, standing right here in front of her. In Shannon's cottage.

Her mother was dressed in crisp linen slacks, a silk blouse, and heels. Not exactly beachwear. Not a hint of the gray hair she surely had by now was showing in her flawlessly arranged hairdo. Her nails shone with a perfect manicure on her long, slender fingers. A gold bracelet resided next to her designer watch.

Molly pushed her wayward lock of hair back… the one with a trace of gray… and glanced down at her toenails with a bit of chipped polish on her left big toe. Her mother carefully looked her over, no doubt taking in her shortcomings.

Her mother finally noticed Wade. "Ah, I didn't know you'd come here with some young man. You should have told me." Her mom frowned, then looked closely at Wade, obviously sizing him up.

She sent Wade an apologetic glance. "Mom, it's not some man. It's Wade Connelly."

"Wait… Wade?" Her mother walked over to him, running her gaze from the top of his head down to his sandaled feet.

"Yes, ma'am." Wade bobbed his head and reached out his hand.

Her mother took it and shook it slowly. "You look… different."

He laughed. "That's what Molly said."

"I didn't know you two were still friends."

"We aren't." She frowned. "I mean we are. I…" She turned to Wade for help.

"I haven't seen Molly since you two left. Not

176

until she came to Belle Island to clear out Shannon's cottage."

"He's been helping me pack things up." She rushed to explain, trying not to look at him, trying to push away the thoughts of their almost-kiss. She could still feel the heat of a blush on her face and she looked guiltily at her mother, suddenly feeling like a teenager who'd tried to sneak a kiss with a boy.

"I see." Her mother looked at Wade again. "So, you still live on the island?"

"I do. Next door in my parent's house. They moved to a retirement place."

"I see," her mother said again in a tone that said she *didn't* see why anyone would live on the island, then turned back to her. "Then it's okay if I stay here."

It was more of a statement than a question.

"Um, of course. You'll stay for Christmas?" She didn't know how she felt about that. Because she wanted to do all the Christmas things with Wade. They had plans to walk downtown tonight and look at the window displays. The children's choir had a concert at the church one night next week that she wanted to go to. She remembered singing in that very same choir as a young girl. But her mother's idea of Christmas plans was... not doing much celebrating at all. At most, going out to eat on Christmas Eve, then out to eat brunch somewhere on Christmas Day. No real traditions. And her mother hadn't sent her a Christmas present in years, though Molly tried to send her at least a little something each year. A pretty scarf, leather gloves, a book she thought her mom might enjoy. Never a thank you for the gifts, either.

And then there was the kiss to consider. The almost-kiss. That wouldn't happen again with her mother here.

"Yes, I'll stay. I have no other plans." Her mom interrupted her thoughts.

Not a ringing endorsement of enthusiasm or wanting to really be here with her. Just the only option she had at this time.

Suddenly, all her plans and her excitement about the coming week crumbled into tiny kernels of missed opportunities.

"And why in the world do you have all these Christmas decorations up? You'll just have to take them all down. Aren't you getting the cottage ready for sale?"

She glanced at Wade, then back at her mother, and shrugged. "I wanted to have one last Christmas here. Complete with a tree and decorations. One last memory of Christmas here on Belle Island."

Her mother sent her a look that said she disapproved, but that was nothing new. She was used to those looks.

Wade cleared his throat. "I should go. Let you two catch up."

"You don't have to go." Did her voice sound pleading?

He looked at her questioningly.

"Molly, let the young man go. I'm sure he has better things to do than help you clear out Shannon's house. Goodbye, Wade. Nice to see you."

Summarily dismissed, Wade nodded. "I'll talk to you soon, Molls." He sent her an apologetic glance and ducked out the door.

Traitor.

But at least this would give her a chance to talk to her mother. The anger that she'd tamped down crept back up to the surface. "I'm actually glad you came, Mom." And in a way, she was. Now she could confront her in person.

"I'm sure we'll have a pleasant Christmas."

Pleasant. Just what everyone wanted. A *pleasant* Christmas.

"My suitcase is in the car. Would you mind getting it for me?"

"Sure." So she was the bellman, too? She headed out to the car. Two suitcases and a leather tote bag, actually. Her mother never traveled lightly. She tugged them up the stairs and into the house. "Do you want to stay in your old room or in Shannon's?"

Her mother frowned. "Shannon's, I guess. It has the private bathroom, and it's much larger than the cramped guest room I used to stay in."

She put the suitcases in Shannon's room and returned. "So, I was just having a glass of wine. Would you like one?"

"What kind it is?"

"Cabernet."

"A good one?"

"Good enough." She turned and headed to the kitchen. No doubt this wouldn't be a satisfactory bottle in her mother's opinion, but she didn't care. She poured the glass and headed back to hand it to her mother.

Her mother made a slight face after she took

her first tiny sip, but Molly ignored it. "Mom, sit down. I want to talk to you."

Her mother perched on the edge of a worn, overstuffed chair. Molly went over to the bookcase and picked up the ornament resting on a shelf. She slowly turned and walked over to her mother. "I found this."

The color drained out of her mother's face, but she quickly covered up her surprise and asked innocently, "What's that?"

"An ornament. It was in a box of things Shannon kept. The box was labeled Regina."

"Hm, I don't remember it."

"No idea who J is?" She thrust the ornament into her mother's hand.

Her mother turned it over, tracing the words on the back. Two bright pink spots dotted her cheeks. "I really have no idea."

She stood with her hands on her hips, facing her mother. "And yet I think you do."

Her mother shook her head.

"I think it's from my father."

Her eyes widened, and she looked up, unable to cover her surprise this time.

"Not the fictional one you said died when I was a baby. My real father. The one you never told me I had. James Jones." The words came out in harsh stabs of pain and anger.

"I—"

She held up her hand. "Don't lie to me. Don't even try. How could you keep this from me?"

"How did you find out?"

"Shannon left me a letter. Told me."

"Shannon should have minded her own business." She shook her head. "It wasn't her secret to tell."

"It wasn't yours to keep all these years," she rebutted. "I had a right to know the truth."

Her mother placed the ornament on the table next to her. "It... It was easier this way."

"Easier?" Fury choked her, and she balled her hands into fists. "Easier for you, maybe. But not for me. Not for my father."

"You don't know what it was like to be unmarried and pregnant back then. Shannon moved away with me and we got an apartment as far away from Hays, Kansas, as we could so no one would know. No one would gossip. We both worked, and she helped me with you. Then we came up with the idea to say your father had died."

"But why keep him from knowing about me?"

"He moved away from Hays. How was I to find him? Do you know how many James Joneses there are out there? And we didn't have the easy access to everyone and everything with the internet like now. It was just easier to keep things the way they were. And he was a young man then. He wouldn't want to be saddled with a child."

Saddled with a child. Nice. Is that how her mother thought about her? But, of course, she did. They'd never been close, and her mother had been relieved when she'd gone away to college.

"But you never gave him a choice, did you?"

"I did what I thought was best."

"But why not tell me after I was older? We could have looked for him now that there are better resources for finding people."

"What good would that do?"

"I could meet him. Get to know my father." Anger swept through her, drowning her with its intensity. Did her mother not see how wrong keeping this secret was? How much it hurt her?

"It wouldn't change anything."

"Mom, there are times I don't understand you." Like most of the time. "He's my father. I want to know him."

"We don't even know where he is. If he's alive."

"I'm going to try and find him. I *will* find him."

"It won't do any good. What's done is done. And he'd be shocked if you told him now. Angry."

"Like I'm angry?" She gritted her teeth. "You're not even sorry about the lie, are you?"

"I did what I thought was right. What I had to do. I couldn't have people gossiping about me," her mother said defiantly and rose from the chair. "I'm tired from the trip. I think I'll go unpack and lie down."

"Shannon left you a letter, too." Molly walked over to the bookcase, grabbed the letter, and thrust it at her mother.

She just looked down at it, not taking it.

"Mom, take the letter." She shoved it into her mother's hand. "Don't you want to read it? Know what she said?"

"There's nothing left to be said." Her mom crossed the room, shoved the letter into her purse, and disappeared into Shannon's bedroom.

She scooped up her glass of wine, her hands shaking, and went to stand by the window, staring out at the water. Anger swirled along with sadness. So much had happened in the last weeks. But this cottage would be gone soon. It was probably for the best that the kiss with Wade was interrupted. She'd just been lost in the moment. The thrill of winning the baking contest. The happiness of being back on Belle Island. How comfortable and familiar it was to be with him.

But all this was ending. This magical fantasy life she'd been living since she got here. Magical except for the part where she learned she had a father. A living one. Hopefully, a living one. She wanted to find him. She would find him. And it was magical in a way to at least have a chance.

She stood by the window for a long time, watching the sun slowly set below the horizon and the first stars twinkle in the sky. Exhaustion finally overwhelmed her. She washed out the wine glasses—her mother's barely touched—and set them to dry on the drying rack. She made coffee for the morning and set it to come on at six. She looked at the familiar clock, the radio on the counter, the same wooden table and closed her eyes, memorizing every detail. Then she walked out of the kitchen and flicked off the light, searing the memory in her mind to pull out later when the cottage was gone.

CHAPTER 20

The next morning, Molly stood out on the deck, sipping on her first cup of coffee. She wrapped her hands around the mug's warmth, watching the sky lighten in the distance.

Someone walking on the beach in the distance caught her eye, and as they got closer, she realized it was Wade. He waved when he saw her, crossed the beach, and jogged up to her deck.

"Hey, you. You doing okay?" He lounged against the railing.

"Not really. My mother is..." She closed her eyes, then opened them. "She's impossible."

"So you talked to her last night?"

"I did. Showed her the ornament. At first, she pretended she had no idea what it was."

"But she eventually told you about your father?"

"No, I had to tell her I knew the truth. That James Jones is my father. That Shannon told me. Her answer was to be angry with Shannon for telling me."

"So did you eventually talk things out?"

"Oh, we talked. Or I talked. She just made excuses. No apology and she doesn't want me to try to find my father. But I'm going to, no matter if she likes it or not."

"I'll help you." He reached out and took her hand. "I'm sorry everything has been so… confusing… these last weeks."

"It has. I didn't realize how much I missed the island. Missed Shannon—but now it's too late to do anything about that. Then I find out I have a father. It's all too much."

He pushed her rebellious lock of hair back from her face. She really should get a haircut that did something about that silly lock of hair. And why was she thinking about haircuts now?

"I didn't help things last night, did I?"

She looked into his eyes, remembering their

near-miss kiss. "I was just caught up in the moment. Thrilled to win the contest. Remembering our good times here on the island."

"Is that all it was?"

"Yes," she said definitively. Or as definitively as she could when she was uncertain. "Our timing is off. Wrong. It's just too much for me to deal with along with everything else. Besides, I just got dumped by Roger. I need time."

He looked at her with sad eyes. "You know I'll do anything you want. Give you time. Just be friends." He squeezed her hand. "But please don't disappear for years again. Let's at least still stay friends. I'd miss you too much if you just slip out of my life again."

"We can try. But you know how that goes. Distance is the mortal enemy of relationships."

"It doesn't have to be. You can come back here and visit."

"I could. Maybe. But I think it would hurt too much. Being here but not having the cottage. All my memories of here are so bittersweet. They almost choke me when I think of how it could have been. If only Mom would have listened to Shannon. Told me about my father way back then. If we'd kept coming back here each year."

"Life doesn't always go according to how we'd like it to, does it?"

"No, it doesn't." She turned away from his wistful gaze and looked out at the sea.

"We still have this year. Lots of things planned. We'll have fun," he said with forced cheerfulness.

"Yes, we do." She turned back to him. "And I'll try not to let my mom ruin any of our plans. I want the full Belle Island Christmas experience. The children's concert, window shopping downtown. Oh, and can we do a bonfire on the beach like we used to? Roast marshmallows and make s'mores?"

"We can do anything you want. I promise to give you a Christmas to remember."

She smiled, trying to match his cheerfulness. The thing was, he'd already given her a Christmas to remember. One that she'd take with her and pull out each memory, carefully unwrapping it like the present it was.

Molly stepped inside the cottage and found her mother pouring a cup of coffee. "Morning, Mom."

"Good morning." Her mother turned to her. "I've decided it would be best if I pack up and leave."

"Mom, you don't have to do that."

"I think, due to the circumstances, it's the prudent thing to do. I can't change your mind about looking for your father. Don't blame me if it blows up in your face. Even if you somehow find him, I'm not sure what you'll gain out of it. He might not even accept you as his daughter."

"Or he might. We might have a chance at some kind of relationship."

"Molly, you've always lived in some kind of fantasy world. Sometimes life just… isn't fair."

She swallowed, still holding back her anger. But she didn't want her mother to leave. At least not like this. "You should stay for Christmas. You don't have any other plans."

"I'm sure I can find some Christmas parties to attend back home."

Why was she trying so hard to have her mother stay? She would only ruin all her Christmas plans. All the things she wanted to do with Wade. Though now that she and Wade had made the decision to just be friends, her mother would make a good buffer.

"No, I've made up my mind. I'm going to pack my things, then I'm leaving."

"You don't have to." She tried one more time, not sure that she truly wanted her to change her mind. Did that make her a terrible daughter?

Her mom just shook her head and disappeared into her bedroom.

Thirty minutes later she reappeared, dragging her own suitcases this time, with the tote bag thrown over one of the handles. "Goodbye, Molly. I hope you have a nice Christmas."

"Mom… are you sure you want to go?"

"Yes." She bobbed her head.

"At least let me help with the luggage."

She relinquished both suitcases, and Molly carried them out to the car and put them in the back seat. She started to give her mother a hug but pulled back. As her mother always said, they weren't a hugging family.

"And here, you keep the ornament. I don't

want it." Her mom thrust the ornament into her hands.

She glanced at the silver heart. Her mother couldn't hide from the truth by leaving the ornament behind.

Her mother slid gracefully into the car, gave a wave of her perfectly manicured hand, and pulled out of the drive.

She sank down on the front step, feeling lost and abandoned but not sure why. It wasn't like she usually spent Christmas with her mom. They hadn't spent a Christmas together in years. Feeling abandoned was just... silly. She turned the ornament over in the palm of her hands, reading the words again.

Merry Christmas, you have my heart. J.

Was he heartbroken when her mother up and disappeared? Had he really loved her?

She jumped back up. There was only one thing that would help at a time like this.

Baking.

She'd just run to the market and get more supplies. A person could never do enough Christmas baking. Ever.

CHAPTER 21

Molly went into town and took a walk along Oak Street before picking up her groceries. It was a nice day out, and people bustled along the sidewalk, ducking in and out of stores and calling out Christmas greetings.

Strangers stopped and congratulated her on winning the baking contest. She felt like part of the town. Like she belonged. She had to admit, it was a nice feeling. Though it would be short-lived, she reminded herself.

She passed by a gift shop and Julie came hurrying out. "Hi, Molly," Julie said as she adjusted the packages she was carrying.

"Hi. Looks like you've been doing some shopping."

"I have. Needed to pick up some gifts for my employees. And I found the perfect gift for Tally. It's a new book out with old photos and the history of Belle Island. Lots of her relatives from generations back are in it."

"Oh, I bet she'll love that."

"I've been having a run on my cinnamon scones at The Sweet Shoppe." Julie laughed. "It always pays to win the baking contest. Draws in new people to the restaurant."

"They were delicious."

A couple walked past, smiled, and congratulated both of them. Julie's lips tipped up in a grin. "Been getting a lot of that."

"Me, too. I didn't realize so many people knew who I was."

"Everybody knows everybody and everything here on Belle Island. No secrets." Julie switched her bags to her other hand and glanced at her watch. "I better run. Need to get back to The Sweet Shoppe."

Julie hurried off down the street and Molly headed down the sidewalk. Christmas was in full swing here in town. Music drifted out from the open shop doors. She loved being here at Christmastime. She'd forgotten how festive it was. How friendly the people were. How the town went all out for the holidays. Even with all the recent drama, she was having the best time.

She was going to have much more than the *pleasant* Christmas her mother said they'd have. She was going to have a wonderful Christmas. A marvelous Christmas. A Christmas so very much better than a *pleasant* one.

With a smile firmly in place, she hurried off to the market to get her baking supplies. An afternoon of baking could only make the day better.

After trying and failing to concentrate on work for a client, Wade snapped the laptop shut, got up, and wandered around his house. He picked up stray coffee cups that always seemed to appear all over his home. He was forever pouring a cup, forgetting where he set it down, and pouring a new one. He adjusted the garland over the bookcase. Picked up a throw pillow that had fallen to the floor. Folded the afghan from his mother.

Melancholy hovered around him,

smothering him in a blanket of loneliness. A loneliness filled with haunting if-onlys regarding Molly. If only her mother and Shannon hadn't fought. If only he and Molly had kept in contact. If only her mother hadn't shown up last night, interrupting them. If only he'd been able to kiss her. Finally. After all these years. And something he'd been wanting to do since the first day she'd returned with her warm brown eyes, friendly smile, and that one adorable curl of hair that hung in her eyes and drove her crazy. He loved touching its softness, pushing it back from her face so he could see directly into her eyes.

Just like he had right before they'd almost kissed.

But it was all too much for her. She'd said that. They would just be friends, even if that's not exactly what he wanted. But he wanted Molly to feel safe and happy more than anything. More than he wanted what *he* wanted.

All the reasons they shouldn't be together played like a litany through his mind. He walked over to the Christmas tree and took off an ornament made of twisted pipe cleaners, bent slightly out of shape over the years. A battered tag hung from it. *Merry Christmas from Molly* was scrawled in childish handwriting. He remembered making these with her one year. They had to have been about six. And he still kept the one she gave him.

He pulled out his phone and scrolled through the photos he'd taken of them the other night. Molly laughing up at him. Making silly faces. Hugging him. Soon, that would be all he had left of these weeks together.

But he planned on making every moment they had left count. Make this the best Christmas ever for Molly. Even if it would shred him to pieces when she left. He wouldn't think about that now. He'd only think about making the next days special for her. Though he guessed that would now include her mother, and she'd made it fairly clear that she wasn't his biggest fan. She'd been like that all those years ago, too. Shannon had accepted him as almost family, but Regina? She'd always been standoffish with him. Not much he could do except try to win her over now.

A knock sounded, and he hurried to the

door, hoping it was Molly. But a man stood there looking slightly out of place with long pants, leather shoes, and a long-sleeved button-up dress shirt—albeit he had the sleeves rolled up.

"I'm sorry to bother you, but I'm looking for Shannon. No one's answering at her house. She still lives next door?" He glanced back over his shoulder toward Shannon's house.

"Ah… are you a friend of hers?"

"Yes, from long ago."

He paused, hating to give the news. "I'm sorry to say that Shannon passed away a few months ago."

"No." The man's eyes filled with sadness and disappointment. "That's too bad. I wanted to speak with her."

"I'm sorry."

"I just got this letter from her. Forwarded to my new address. She wrote to me and said she had something important to tell me."

Wade looked at him skeptically, but a tiny kernel of hope grew inside him. "And your name?"

The man smiled. "Oh, sorry. Didn't

introduce myself. Jim. Jim Jones." He held out his hand.

A wide grin spread across Wade's face. "Well, Mr. Jones. Come inside. Let me get you a drink. I've got someone who is dying to meet you."

CHAPTER 22

Molly got home and hauled in a load of groceries, setting them on the counter. She headed back for another load and walked inside, juggling the last three bags. A knock sounded, and she heard Wade call out. "Molly, it's Wade."

She went to the front of the house, adjusting the bags of groceries so she had a hand to open the door. Why was Wade at the front door? He usually came to the back.

She tugged the door open, careful not to drop any of her bags.

"Hey, Molls." His eyes sparkled with eagerness.

"Hi." She looked at him questioningly. A

man stood beside him and gave her a friendly smile.

"I have someone I want to introduce to you." Wade's face flushed with excitement.

Her brows furrowed. What was going on? Who was this man? Oh, maybe Wade's investigator friend.

"Molly, this is…" Wade paused, looking at her intensely. "This is Jim Jones."

She stepped back, dropping her bags. It barely registered that they crashed to the floor. Wade stepped inside quickly and caught a pair of oranges rolling across the floor. She blinked and stared at the man.

Jim Jones. She couldn't find a word to say.

Wade motioned for the man to come inside. "Jim came looking for Shannon, but I told him she'd passed. But I said there was someone who'd love to meet him."

She stared at Wade, then at the man. "Did you tell him?"

"No, I figured that was yours to tell. Or Regina's."

"Regina Croft? Shannon's best friend?" Jim asked, his eyes widening in surprise.

"Yes, she's… my mother." She looked at Wade quickly.

"How is Regina? I haven't seen her in years. She and Shannon just up and left town when we all were young. I was so surprised. I… ah… I dated Regina."

"My mother left this morning."

Wade's eyes flashed in surprise at that piece of news. They all stood there awkwardly until Wade said, "Jim, why don't you come in? Molly, we should probably all sit down."

She looked at Wade gratefully and led them over to the sofa. The man—why was she still thinking of him as *the man*—settled comfortably into the overstuffed chair and Wade sat on the sofa beside her. He nodded encouragingly at her. "Go ahead. It's yours to tell."

She looked at the m—Jim Jones—and swallowed. How does one tell a complete stranger that he's your father? The father of a child he never knew existed. Only she wasn't a child anymore.

She sucked in a deep breath. "Shannon never had any children, and she left her cottage to me when she died. So that's why I'm here."

"Not surprising. Shannon and Regina were

always so close. Almost like sisters." Jim flashed a congenial smile.

"I did call her Aunt Shannon when I was young. But Shannon and my mother had a falling out."

"They did? Over what? I can't imagine that." Jim frowned.

"Over… you."

His eyes widened in surprise. "Me?"

"I don't know how to make this any easier, so I'm just going to say it." She paused, gathering courage, her heart pounding. "It seems…"

Wade nodded at her, his eyes filled with support.

"You're my father," she blurted the words out.

"What?" Jim shoved himself out of the chair.

She stood. "I just found out. Shannon left me a letter and told me."

"Shannon left a letter?"

"Yes, she thought I should know the truth. She always thought that, I guess. That's what they argued about years ago. The fight that tore apart their friendship. She wanted my mom to tell you and tell me."

Jim looked over at her as if memorizing her every feature. "You're my daughter?" he asked softly.

"Yes."

"I can't believe it." He walked over to her and put his hand on her arm. "My daughter."

She stared into his warm brown eyes. "I know. I was surprised, too. I was told my father died when I was a baby. But now... you're standing right here."

"I can see the resemblance," Wade said. "Look at you two. Same shade of brown eyes, same nose and chin."

She stared at her father's face, looking for similarities. She had to admit she had his same square chin, same strong jawline. Nothing like her mother's delicate features and blue eyes.

"I wish Regina would have told me." His voice cracked. "I've missed all these years with you. I would have married her. Or at least been there for her if she didn't want marriage. I was madly in love with her. And she just... disappeared. Left me a note that I found after she was gone that said she and Shannon were moving away and striking out on their own. She wanted a clean slate for that. She didn't tell me where they went. I was devastated at the time."

"I guess Shannon was the only one who knew the truth. Besides my mom, of course."

"You think that's why Shannon wrote to me? She was going to tell me?"

"I think so. Her letter to me said she'd been trying to find you. I can't believe Mom hid this from me." Tears began to roll down her cheeks as she choked on her emotions.

Her father opened his arms, and she walked into them. "My daughter," he whispered as he held her close. "I'm so grateful for finding you."

She stepped back and swiped at her eyes, seeing his eyes glisten with unshed tears. "I don't know what's next. Do you want to take a DNA test or something?"

He shook his head. "No, that's not needed. I see myself in you. And one thing I'm sure about. Regina would not have been with someone else while we were dating. She wasn't like that. I thought… well, I thought I might ask her to marry me once we graduated."

"I don't understand why she didn't tell you."

"I wish she had. I guess she was scared of

being the unwed pregnant girl. Things were different back then. There was one pregnant girl in our class and people were always whispering about her. Sad, really. But Regina would not have wanted to be that girl. She always glowed with a radiant force. People loved her. She was funny, and witty, and always the center of attention."

"That doesn't make it right though. Doesn't excuse her. And even if she was scared to tell you when it happened, she could have told you later. After she had me. She made some lame excuse that you'd moved away from Hays."

"I did move away. Right after Regina and Shannon left. I couldn't stand to still be there. See the places we hung out. Too many memories. Left and got a good job, then put myself through engineering school, then got my master's with the help of some scholarships."

"Mom was here last night. I told her I knew. That I wanted to find you. She was so against telling you. She left this morning after I insisted I was looking for you. She was afraid that you'd reject me. Not believe it."

"Ah, no. I believe you. I do. And I couldn't be more pleased. I'm sorry for all the years I've missed. Not knowing you. Not seeing you grow up. But I'm very pleased that we at least have the chance now to know each other. There's so much I want to know about you. About your life." He laughed. "I want to know every detail."

"How about you two go to Magic Cafe and grab an early dinner? You can talk," Wade suggested.

She turned to him. "Wade, you have to come with us."

"You sure?"

"I'm sure. Please."

"Yes, do come with us," Jim said.

Jim. What should she call this man? She guessed Jim was as good as anything. At least for now.

CHAPTER 23

Tally looked up from the hostess station to see Molly, Wade, and another gentleman with them. "Good evening. Great to see you again."

"Hi, Tally. This is my father."

"Oh, nice to meet you." Tally was a bit confused because she was certain she'd heard Molly's father had died when she was just a tiny baby.

"Jim Jones." The man reached out his hand and she shook it, surprised.

Jim Jones. The name on the envelope she'd mailed for Shannon. "Oh—"

Molly looked at her closely. "Did you know?"

Tally shook her head. "No, but I mailed a letter for Shannon. Jim Jones was the name on it. She just told me she was trying to right a wrong."

"That letter found me. Eventually. I'd moved, but it was forwarded. I'm very grateful you mailed it for her. And that Shannon wrote to me."

He turned and smiled at Molly. "Because today I found out I have a daughter I never knew about. And I'm very thankful."

"And that story that Mom told everyone? That my father died when I was a baby. As you can see, not all truths are exactly as they seem." Molly shook her head. "I'm so grateful Shannon told me the truth."

"And found me." Jim smiled at Molly, looking thoroughly pleased.

"I'm happy for both of you." Tally looked at Molly beaming beside her father.

Though there was no sign of Regina with them and she wondered how that was going to shake out. Was this what had caused the rift between Regina and Shannon? Well, it wasn't hers to meddle in. But she was truly happy for Molly.

"How about a table by the beach? Looks like we're in for a spectacular sunset tonight. And I'll send over a bottle of champagne. Seems like you all have a lot to celebrate."

They all sat down and toasted with their champagne, then Jim started in with questions. "Where do you live?"

"I live in Denver. I'm loving avoiding winter down here in Florida. Where do you live?"

"I just moved from Montana to—get this —Orlando."

"Oh, wow. That's only a couple of hours from here."

"It is."

"Are you planning on driving back tonight? You should stay with me. At the cottage."

"Oh, thank you. But I booked a room at Belle Island Inn for a few nights. Very nice place. Met the owner, Susan. Wonderful lady. I have a room overlooking the gulf. Belle Island is such a beautiful place. I can see why Shannon decided to settle here."

"I'm going to call Mom tonight when I get

home. I'm going to tell her you're here if that's okay."

"I…" His forehead wrinkled. "Yes, of course. She's your mother. I just don't know how I feel about seeing her now. She's kept you from me for all these years. I've missed out on… on everything. Your first smile, first steps, first day of school… and everything else that has happened to you."

"I'm going to invite her to come back here. But I don't know that she will. She's… stubborn."

He gave a wry laugh. "Yes, she is. I remember that from when we were dating. Once she makes her mind up, there's no changing it."

"I'm going to at least try and see if she'll come back. I know it will be awkward, but maybe we all could talk." She sighed. "I don't know what I want or what I think might happen."

"It's all very confusing now, isn't it?" Jim's eyes lit up. "But I'm so glad I know the truth now. I hope we can have some kind of relationship now, whatever we can make it."

"I'd like that very much." She looked at him. "So… do you have plans for Christmas?"

"No, not really. I was just going to go to the club for their Christmas brunch."

"You should stay for Christmas." She paused. "But I didn't even ask. Do you have a wife? Family?"

"I have an ex-wife. I married when I was thirty-five. My wife didn't want any kids, but I didn't find out that pertinent piece of information until we'd been married for ten years and she told me she wanted a divorce."

"I'm sorry."

"Ah, that's okay. Life lessons. I have a good life. I've got two nephews and a niece I see often."

"So, you could stay for Christmas?"

His brow puckered with concentration, then his lips tipped into a smile. "I'd like that very much."

"Great." She clapped her hands. "We have so many plans. The children's concert, window shopping. It's just magical here at Christmas."

"We? I didn't ask if you're married. I just assumed since you're here alone…"

"No, I'm not married. We. That's Wade and me." She smiled at Wade and he flashed a smile back at her. "He's my good friend. I've known him since I was a little girl and Mom and I would come to Belle Island each summer and each Christmas."

"Until the argument?"

"Until then. I'd never been back until after Shannon died. I regret that. I found out when I was clearing out her cottage that she'd written tons of letters to me. My mom always marked them return to sender. I wish I'd known."

"Looks like Regina kept a lot of secrets."

"She has, and I have so much anger and resentment toward her now. I'll have to find a way to deal with that. I'm not sure I can ever forgive her. I don't blame you if you can't forgive her, either."

Jim leaned back in his chair. "I'm not really one for holding grudges, though I have to admit, I do feel a simmering anger toward Regina that she kept you from me." He shrugged. "I'll have to work through that, too."

"I guess we both will." Wanting to change the subject, she turned to asking him questions, and they spent the evening getting to know each other. His absolute love of all things baseball.

His eclectic music choices of jazz, country, classic rock. He'd lived in ten different cities since he graduated from college with a master's in engineering.

She told him about her work, where she'd lived, and that she too, loved jazz and knew nothing really about baseball. He promised he'd take her to a baseball game someday and explain it to her.

And just like that, they were making plans for the future.

Jim left for the inn after they finished dinner and Wade sat out on Molly's deck with her. She sipped a cup of chamomile tea, trying to settle her nerves. Though it didn't really look like it was working.

"Been quite the day, hasn't it?" Wade asked as he stretched his long legs out and leaned back in the comfortable chair, sipping on a beer.

"My mind is spinning. This week has been such a whirlwind of surprises."

"You doing okay?" He looked over at her, concerned. "It's really been a lot."

"I think I'm okay. I mean, it will take a bit to process it all. First, finding out about my father and the secret Mom hid from me. Then for him to actually show up here. What are the chances?"

"Kind of like fate decided to give you both a nudge, isn't it?"

She looked at him thoughtfully. "It is kind of like that."

"I'm glad he's staying for Christmas. That will give you both some time together."

"It will. And Christmas with Jim and with you, all here on Belle Island. That sounds wonderful."

"You think your mom might come back?"

"I don't know. I'll call her in the morning. I can't really face calling her tonight. But I'm going to ask her to come back to the island. What she does from there is up to her, and I'll just have to make peace with her decision."

Molly sat, staring out at the water, sipping her tea, lost in thought. He sat silently beside her, just wanting to be there for her.

She finally turned back to him. "Jim seems like a really nice guy."

"He does."

"He didn't even question that I'm his daughter."

"It would be hard to. You look a lot like him."

"I do, don't I? I think that's nice. I always looked at my mother and couldn't see a bit of a resemblance to her." She set her cup down, empty now. "I should probably head in. I'm exhausted."

"No wonder. It's been quite the week." He rose. "I'll hope you can get a good night's sleep."

"My mind is racing. I'd hoped the chamomile might help. Maybe I'll take a nice long soak in the tub with a good book."

He nodded. Getting lost in a good book was a standard Molly move. It would probably help her relax. He stepped off the deck. "I'll check in with you tomorrow, but call me if you need anything. Or if you just want to talk. Even if it's late tonight or early morning."

"I will." She nodded and headed inside, leaving him standing in the sand. He trudged over to his cottage and slipped in the back door, flipping on the switch that turned on the

Christmas tree lights. A low glow filled the room.

He walked over and sat on the sofa, feeling lonely. Which was ridiculous because he'd lived alone for years. What was different about tonight?

Oh, he knew what was different. He'd gotten used to spending his time with Molly, not alone. Even his beloved Christmas decorations did little to lift his spirits.

CHAPTER 24

Molly tried her mother's phone the next morning, but she didn't pick up. It figured. Her mother was probably not speaking to her. Or it was too early for her to be up. She debated leaving a message but decided against it. If she kept calling often enough, surely her mother would pick up, wouldn't she?

She'd made plans to meet her father for breakfast at the inn, so she hurried to get ready, deciding on navy capris and a crisp white top. Shorts sounded too casual and a dress too fancy, though why she was so worried about what to wear escaped her. She was just having breakfast. She had just enough time to walk, so she hurried outside and headed down the street.

She was going to meet *her father* for breakfast. Just like a normal person. She hummed a Christmas tune softly as she walked along, feeling like her life was on an exciting new path. One that included a father. A parent who actually wanted to spend time with her. A startling difference from how her mother had always treated her. As an afterthought. Never making her a priority. She pushed the thoughts away and settled back on happy thoughts of finding her father.

She walked into the inn and saw him standing by the reception desk. She crossed over quickly and was met with his welcoming smile.

"Molly, good morning," he said, his voice full of warmth. "This is Susan. She owns the hotel. Do you know her? Susan, this is my daughter, Molly."

"No, I don't think we've met. Hello, Susan."

"Nice to meet you, Molly. Rumor has it that you're the winner of the bake contest."

"Well, I tied with Julie."

"You both deserved the win. Both entries were excellent."

"Thank you." She blushed under the

compliments. Did everyone in town know about the baking contest win?

"Are you ready for breakfast?" Jim asked.

At least she was over thinking of him as *the man*… "I am."

She followed him into the dining room, and they settled at a table by the window. After ordering, they sat and sipped on coffee. He liked his black just like she did. She loved picking up on little details of ways they were similar.

"So, what are your plans for today?" he asked.

"I thought I'd do some shopping. I want to get Wade a Christmas present. And I always get Mom something. I guess I'll mail it off to her if she doesn't come back here. I called her, but she didn't answer."

"I have to admit, my curiosity is up just thinking about seeing her again."

"Even after what she did? Not telling you about me?"

"Even after that. I'm more sad than angry about it, I think. I wish she'd told me. I really wish that. But I kind of understand. Times were different then. Doesn't make it right, but does put it in perspective."

"She could have told you later. Or when I got a bit older."

"She could have. But she didn't. I'm not going to let my life be run by if-onlys. I'm going to be grateful we have each other now. Holding a grudge only hurts the person holding it."

Her father was wiser than she was. More forgiving. She should be more like him. *Holding a grudge only hurts the person holding it.* That was so true. Maybe she could find a way to forgive her mother. Maybe.

The waitress delivered two plates of French toast smothered in syrup and powdered sugar with a side of bacon. He loved French toast, too. Just like she did. Another similarity.

They ate their breakfast, asking a million more questions. Favorite color. Favorite holiday. Favorite dessert.

When they finished, Jim walked her out to the expansive front porch. "I'm glad you could join me for breakfast."

"Yes, it was nice." Her first breakfast ever with her father. They had a lot of firsts ahead of them. "How about you come over to the cottage for dinner tonight? I'd love to cook for you.

Shannon taught me all my cooking skills. It was something we'd do together each year."

"I'd love that."

"Then Wade and I were going to head downtown and look at the Christmas lights. Want to come with us?"

"Yes, that sounds great."

"Perfect. About six?"

"I'll be there."

She headed out down the sidewalk and looked back to see him still standing there. She gave a wave and turned the corner. She'd have to come up with something special for dinner tonight. And she'd ask Wade to come, too. Which reminded her. She still needed to find the perfect Christmas gift for him.

Once again, she hummed a holiday song as she hurried back home.

No, not *home.*

She corrected herself. Back to *the cottage.*

CHAPTER 25

Molly decided to make a dish Shannon called shipwreck stew that had delicious flavors in it. She remembered it well. She made homemade rolls and a fresh salad to go along with it. Then she baked both a pecan pie and a peach pie because she couldn't decide between the two of them.

She called her mother two more times. Still, she didn't pick up. She'd left one message saying she really need to talk to her. She'd just keep calling. Surely her mom would see all the missed calls and call her back, or at least pick up out of curiosity, if for no other reason.

The day cooled off with an upcoming

storm, so she changed into slacks and a lightweight sweater. The kitchen clock ticked off the minutes as she set the table, washed up the dishes from her baking, and put them away. The heady aroma of the beef stew mixed with the sweet smell of freshly baked rolls, pecans, cinnamon, and peaches.

It was silly to be nervous about having her father to dinner, but she was. Wade had thankfully accepted her invitation, too. Not that Wade ever turned down her cooking. But he was so easy to be with, and she wanted him here for her first dinner she made for her dad.

Wade poked his head in the back door about ten minutes early. "Molls?"

"Hey, come on in." She turned from hanging a dishtowel and took one last glance around the kitchen, making sure it was all nice and tidy.

"I know I'm early, but I was tired of pacing my deck, waiting for six. Oh, and what do I smell? Is that Shannon's stew?"

"It is. Do you remember it?"

"I do, and I also remember how much I love it." Wade lounged against the counter. "Any news from your mom?"

"She hasn't picked up." She shrugged. "And I don't want to leave a message. Though maybe I'll have to resort to that if she doesn't pick up soon."

The doorbell rang, and she went to answer it. Jim stood there holding a bouquet of flowers in one hand and a bottle of wine in the other.

"Oh, thank you." She reached for the flowers. "Come in."

He stepped inside, looking a bit uneasy. Was he as nervous as she was?

"Hi, Jim." Wade came in from the kitchen.

"Good evening. I brought some red wine. Hope that's okay. Whatever you're cooking smells delicious."

"It's Shannon's shipwreck stew. So good." Wade's eyes shone in anticipation.

She took the wine and glanced at the label. One of her favorite wines. The one she'd served her mother the other night. Her mother always turned up her nose at her choice of wines. She assumed that pricier bottles of wine were better, but Molly always went with what she loved. And her favorite red wine was reasonably priced. One other thing she had in common with her dad.

Wade took the bottle, opened it, and poured them all glasses. They went out to sit on the deck and wait for dinner to be ready.

"You're in for a real treat tonight. Molly is the best cook ever. And I saw two pies on the counter. I promise you've never had a better pie than the ones Molly makes."

She laughed. "At least the ones I make now. Not the first one I made when we were kids and you had to choke it down."

"I'm grateful you've improved." Wade laughed.

The doorbell sounded, and she rose. "Better get that. Since I'm staying here longer than I originally planned, I ordered some things I needed online."

She set down her glass and slipped inside, hurrying to the door. Tugging it open, she gasped and stared.

"Mom, what are you doing here?"

"I got your message this morning that you wanted to talk to me and I felt badly about just leaving, though I am right about trying to find your father. That will lead to no good." That was as close as she'd ever heard her mother admit that she might be wrong. But wasn't her mom going to be surprised?

"Well… come in."

Her mother walked past her, into the cottage. "Besides, I really don't have any Christmas plans."

Ah, the no other plans reason. Well, she had a Christmas surprise for her mother.

"Mom, I want to talk to you. Tell you something."

"So you said. But let's have a glass of wine first. It was a long, last-minute trip. Luckily, I hadn't even unpacked my luggage yet."

"I think we should talk first."

"You are always so serious. Always wanting things your way." She shook her head. "A drink first. I need to unwind."

"But, Mom—"

"Molly, do as I say. Get me a glass of wine… though it's probably still that mediocre wine you had the other night. I'll meet you outside. Your house is stifling."

She headed for the deck door and Molly rushed over. "Mom—"

Her mother ignored her and stepped outside. Molly popped out beside her, watching as her mother stood with her mouth open, staring at Jim.

Jim's eyes widened, and he jumped up from his seat. "Regina."

"Jimmy," her mother whispered.

They all stood speechless for a moment. She finally broke the jagged silence. "Uh, Mom decided to come back to spend Christmas on the island."

"What are you doing here?" She still stared at Jim in shock, never taking her eyes off him.

"I got a letter Shannon wrote saying she wanted to talk to me. I came here to find her. But I was sorry to hear she'd passed."

"She shouldn't have written to you," her mother murmured.

"I'm glad she did."

"He came to my house looking for Shannon. I told him there was someone who wanted to meet him." Wade rose from his seat.

They all stood there, staring at each other.

She turned to her mother. "And I told him the truth. That he's my father."

The color drained from her mother's face as she looked between her and Jim.

"You should have told me, Regina. Back

then. When you first found out." Jim stepped toward her mother. "I wouldn't have let you go through it alone."

"I... I couldn't."

"You could have. I would have been there for you."

"The gossip... and Molly would have had the stigma of being born out of wedlock. The way I did it was for the best. No one ever had to know."

"I would have loved to know my daughter as a baby, as a child. Watch her grow up. You took that away from me." Jim stood directly in front of her mother now.

Her mom looked down as if memorizing each detail of the deck planks. "I did what I did. I can't change that."

"You could at least tell him you're sorry." Anger bubbled up inside her. And her mother owed her an apology. But she doubted that either of them would get it.

"I did what I thought I had to do."

Jim took another step and took her mother's hand in his. "I know you did. I understand. I just wish... I wish you would have believed in me. I would have loved to share Molly's life with you."

A lone tear trailed down her mother's face, and Molly stared in disbelief. She'd never seen her mother shed a tear. Not one.

"I wish things had been different," her mother said softly.

That was probably as close to an apology as they were going to get.

She cleared her throat. "Dinner is almost ready. Mom, I'll set another place for you. It's Shannon's shipwreck stew."

"That sounds nice."

"I'll come help you." Wade quickly followed her inside.

She collapsed in a kitchen chair, her hands shaking. Wade dropped to his knees in front of her, taking her hands. "You okay?"

"I will be. I just need a moment. That was... something, wasn't it?"

"It was." He nodded.

"Jim seems to have made peace with what Mom did better than I have. I still have this anger toward her. For everything she took from me."

"You're allowed to feel however you feel,

Molls. It's okay. There's no timeline on getting over something like this."

She let out a long sigh and stood. "You're right. It's going to take me some time. But right now I need to put another place setting out. Get the meal dished up."

Wade stood beside her. "It's going to all be okay, Molls. You'll see."

She stared up at him, her heart swelling with a strange mix of happiness and apprehension. "And you know what I just realized? This is my first ever family dinner."

Molly sat with her mother out on the deck, long after Jim and Wade left. Her mother wasn't even making faces when she took dainty sips of the red wine. She looked lost in thought.

Her mother suddenly turned to her. "Are you ever going to forgive me for what I did?"

She stared at her mother in shock, not used to the brutal honesty. "I… I really don't know."

"I wish you would. I think Jimmy has made peace with it. He understands why I did it. He's

KAY CORRELL

really happy to get the chance to know you now."

"But that doesn't excuse what you did."

"No, it doesn't. But I wish you'd try, for just a moment, to understand my side of it. What I went through. What I was afraid of. A small town and an unmarried young girl. There would have been so much talk. And you would have lived with that talk following you around all the time."

"You could have moved and Jim would have gone with you."

"Maybe. Maybe not. But I honestly thought I was doing the right thing."

"You mean the easiest thing for you."

"You think it was easy moving away from the only place I'd ever known? To a new town where Shannon was the only person I knew? To have you alone?"

She sat back, embarrassed by her lack of empathy. All she'd been thinking about was how all this affected her. Her mother was right. She had no idea how it had been back then. Now unmarried women had children without a lot of gossip surrounding them. A tiny bit of the anger she felt toward her mother began to slip away.

She let out a long sigh. "I just wish you would have told me. Told me at some point in time."

"And maybe I should have. Maybe you're right."

"But I had to hear it from Shannon's letter."

"Shannon always said both you and Jimmy had the right to know the truth. If only I'd listened to her. How different things would have been."

"And we would have kept coming back here to Belle Island. We would have seen Shannon all the time. She would have been a part of my life." She shook her head. "And I found all those letters she wrote to me and you sent back."

"You did?" Her mother looked down at her wine glass before meeting her gaze again. "I am sorry about that. You should have still been able to have a relationship with her. But I was afraid she'd tell you and you'd… you'd hate me."

"Mom, I don't hate you. Not even knowing the truth."

"I wouldn't blame you if you did."

"I don't." She shook her head. "Do I wish you'd told me? Wish I'd been able to know my father back when I was a little kid? Yes, I wish that. But I don't hate you." Another small shard of anger disintegrated into tiny pieces of sand.

Her mother smiled. "I'm glad you don't hate me. I feel…"

"You feel what?"

"I feel like I've always kept my distance from you. To protect myself if you ever found out. If you ever found out and hated me and never forgave me."

"Oh, Mom. What a mess this all is, isn't it?"

"Sometimes the choices we make in life cause a ripple of consequences that we can't even imagine." Her mother's eyes filled with pain. "And my choice about not telling you caused me to lose my best friend."

"What did her letter to you say? Did you read it?"

"I read it. She said she was sorry about the fight. And told me she'd told you about Jimmy and hoped I'd forgive her for that." She paused, looking out at the water. "And she said she loved me and I'd always be her best friend." Her mother choked on the words.

Molly got up and sat beside her mother, wanting to wrap her in a hug but knowing they weren't a hugging family. Instead, she just touched her mother's hand lightly. "I just wish all this could have happened when Shannon was still around. That we could have all been together again."

"So do I," her mother said softly as tears streamed down her face.

CHAPTER 26

The next morning, Wade opened the door to Molly's knock, and she held out arms.

He pulled her close. "You okay, Molls?"

"Mm-hmm." She leaned against him and threaded her arms around his waist. She finally pulled back and grinned up at him. "But I could use a coffee."

He laughed and disappeared, returning with a steaming mug which he pressed into her hands. She sat down on the steps of his deck and he dropped down beside her.

"So Mom and I talked last night. Talked a lot. I think I have a better understanding of what she did. I still wish she'd made different decisions. But… I think I've accepted how it all turned out."

"She's going to stay for Christmas?"

"She is. She even said she'd go to the kids' Christmas choir program tonight. I don't even think she went to it when I was singing in it."

"People change."

"I just can't imagine my mother changing. Though I felt closer to her last night than… well, than I ever have. She went through a lot having me as a single mother."

"And you turned out okay." He bumped his shoulder gently against hers.

"I'm really glad you were here. Still on the island. That you were here for me while I went through all of this."

"I wouldn't want to be anywhere else." He'd do anything to help her and protect her.

She looked up at him. "You're a great friend. You know that?"

His heart pounded at the look in her eyes. "I'll always be here for you, Molls. Whenever you need me." He would be here for her. But how much longer would she be here?

She stared pensively over at Shannon's

cottage, as if taking in every familiar detail. Her eyes clouded for a moment and her brow creased.

Suddenly, she jumped up. "I've got to get home. Mom might be up by now. I'll see you tonight at the children's program? We're going to walk over to it. Can't believe Mom agreed to that. So come over at six thirty, okay?"

"I'll be there."

She leaned over and hugged him. "It's going to be so much fun. The program tonight. And we're still going to make it downtown to see the lights. I have so many plans for this Christmas."

He smiled up at her. "Count me in."

"Oh, I do." She grinned at him. "You're a big part of my plans."

And what did that mean? A big part of her plans. But for how long? Not much longer. Pain sliced through him which he did his best to ignore.

She raced across the sand and hopped up the steps to her deck. With a quick wave back at him, she slipped inside.

The pain he'd tried to ignore roared through him.

That night, they all enjoyed the children's Christmas program and headed outside after it was over. "How about we walk along Oak Street? Look at the lights and the displays in the shop windows?" Molly suggested.

"That sounds like a great idea. Regina, you up for it?" Jim asked.

Her mother nodded. "I think it sounds lovely. If I remember correctly, the town does Christmas up right. Lots of lights and music."

They turned the corner onto Oak Street, and Molly took Wade's arm as her mother and Jim walked a little way in front of them. Jim kept leaning in to say things to her mom, and her laugh rang out numerous times. She couldn't ever remember her mother laughing like that.

Wade nudged her. "Looks like those two are getting along, doesn't it?"

"It does."

"How do you feel about that?"

"I... don't know. Doesn't every child want their parents together? Yet, I'm not a child. And I might be reading too much into this."

She watched as her mother linked her arm with Jim's.

"You never know, Molls. It's Christmas. Surprises happen. Magical things happen at Christmas."

She smiled up at him. "That they do."

CHAPTER 27

The week passed in a whirlwind of activity, hitting all the highlights of Christmas that Belle Island had to offer. One night, Jim and her mother even went out to dinner together at Magic Cafe. Alone.

Jim brought out a side of her mother that she'd never seen. Her mother smiled. Smiled a lot. And was agreeable to all the suggestions of what they would do each night. Molly remembered going to a lot of these Christmas festivities when she was a young girl, but usually just with Shannon. Her mother would often stay back at the cottage. But not this year.

She slipped out of the cottage early Christmas morning and went over to Wade's.

He didn't look a bit surprised to see her and pressed a cup of coffee into her hands. "Merry Christmas, Molls."

"Merry Christmas." She sat on the step of his deck. "I wanted to come see you before all the festivities of the day."

"Yes, my parents should be here in an hour or so. Driving in and staying a few days. Couldn't miss Christmas on Belle Island."

"I wanted some time alone with you."

He eyed her. "You did?"

"Yes... to... give you your present."

He broke into a wide grin. "I love presents."

She laughed. "I know you do. And I think I got one for you this year that you'd never guess."

"Okay, you have my curiosity aroused. What is it?"

She took his hands in hers. "First, I need to say something."

He nodded, squeezing her hands.

"These have been the best weeks. They rival the times we would come to the island when I was a little girl. And... I have really loved spending time with you. Getting to know this older version of Wade."

He tucked that rebellious lock of her hair

back and looked into her eyes. "It's meant everything to me. I'm going to miss you so much when you head back home."

She pursed her lip and tugged a small present out of the pocket of her jacket. "Here, this is for you."

He took the gift and slowly untied the ribbon. She chewed on her lip, waiting for him to finish. He pulled off the wrapping paper and lifted the lid. She held her breath as he picked up a silver ornament.

"Turn it over."

He turned it over, and a wide grin spread across his face. "Do you mean it?"

"Oh, I mean it."

"Merry Christmas, you have my heart. M." He traced his fingers over the inscription. "Ah, Molls, you have my heart, too. You always have." He looked directly into her eyes, and she was certain he was going to kiss her. Finally.

"Morning." Her mother's voice rang out.

She looked over to see her mother out on the deck, waving. "I've got to go. I'll see you over at my house for brunch."

Disappointment crept into Wade's eyes, and he stepped back.

She grinned as she darted home across the sand. Oh, she had more surprises planned for the man.

Molly stood in the kitchen, putting the finishing touches on a huge Christmas brunch. Jim, Wade, her mother, and Wade's parents sat out by the Christmas tree as she checked on everything. The smell of Shannon's coffee cake filled the cottage.

Wade came into the kitchen. "Can I help with anything?"

"No, I've got it. But thanks."

"You look happy." He smiled at her. "I like seeing you like that."

"I am happy." She smiled back at him. "Call everyone in and let's eat."

They all had their brunch, and she glowed at all the compliments on her food. Would she ever get used to family dinners? She loved them. They seemed so strange and yet so normal. Wade's parents treated her like she was part of their lives, in spite of her years away from the island.

"How about I help Molly with the dishes, then we'll open presents?" Wade offered.

"No, let me do the dishes," her mother said.

Molly stared at her in surprise. Her mother was not a dishwashing person. She left her dishes in the sink for her cleaning people to do for her. But she wasn't one to turn down the help. "Okay, if you're sure."

"I'll help Regina." Jim stood up and grabbed his dishes.

She, Wade, and his parents went into the family room and sat by the tree.

"That was the best Christmas meal ever." Wade's father patted his stomach, then turned to his wife. "No offense, dear."

"None taken," Wade's mom said. "Molly takes after Shannon in the cooking department. It was excellent."

She smiled when she heard her mother laughing in the kitchen. Wade leaned close and said softly, "That's nice, isn't it? That they're getting along so well?"

"It is."

Her parents came in and everyone exchanged presents. Christmas music played in the background. The lights on the tree glowed.

Wade held her hand. It was truly a Christmas she'd always remember.

Wade leaned over and grabbed a present. "Here, Molls. This one's for you."

Wondering what he'd gotten her, she took the box and slowly unwrapped it. She gasped in delight when she looked inside. "It's a yellow mixing bowl, just like Shannon's."

"It's *Shannon's* mixing bowl. I went back to the sale when you said you were sorry you donated it. It was already gone, but I found out Julie had bought it. When I explained to her how you wished you'd kept it, she let me have it."

"Oh, it's wonderful." She had to swallow hard to keep back her tears.

"I hoped you'd be pleased."

She gave him a quick peck on the cheek, not failing to notice both their mothers staring at them and smiling.

"And there's one other thing. Something I want to ask." She looked over at Jim. "I was wondering if it would be okay if I called you... Dad."

He jumped up and came over, pulling her to

her feet. "Yes. Yes, it would. That would be the best Christmas present ever."

She grinned at him. "Okay, Dad. Hi, Dad. Merry Christmas, Dad."

They all laughed, and her dad hugged her. "This has been a remarkable Christmas."

"It has." Much better than the *pleasant* Christmas her mother had promised her. It was a magical Christmas.

Wade leaned close and whispered to her. "Best Christmas ever, Molls."

"You can say that again."

"Best Christmas ever," he said as he pulled her close to his side.

CHAPTER 28

Tally, Susan, and Julie sat at Lighthouse Point on Christmas afternoon. Contentment swept through Tally at having this time with her friends. Just the three of them. Oh, they all had husbands they adored, but sometimes a woman just needed time with her friends.

"I swear I've never eaten so much in my life." Tally leaned back. "I loved having Christmas brunch with all of you."

"It was great, wasn't it?" Susan leaned back on her elbows. "I felt like a slacker only providing the fruit and the juices. But then I'd never try to compete with Julie."

"No one competes with Julie," Tally agreed.

"Courtney said you totally spoiled Bobby with gifts this year." Susan looked over at her.

Tally laughed. "I did, and I'm not even sorry about it."

"Of course not. You're his grandmother. It's like part of your job description," Susan said. "And… well… soon I'll be able to spoil my grandchild, too."

"What?" Tally stared at her friend. "Jamie and Cindy are pregnant?"

"They are." Susan practically glowed with the news. "They are keeping it quiet for a bit longer but said I could tell you two. They know we don't keep secrets."

Tally hugged her friend. "I'm so happy for you."

"As long as we don't keep secrets and we're sharing news…" Julie grinned. "Reed and I are going to have a baby, too. Looks like our baby will be growing up with Jamie and Cindy's."

Tally jumped up and pulled Julie to her feet. "That's wonderful news. I couldn't be more pleased."

Susan got up, stood beside them, and wrapped them both in a hug.

Tally stood there at Lighthouse Point, surrounded in a hug from her best friends. Delighting in their good news. For all they'd gone through, for all they still had to share in their future.

"Looks like we don't have to even throw a shell into the water for all our wishes to come true." Tally hugged her friends close, her heart full.

Molly and Wade headed to Lighthouse Point that afternoon, walking off the big Christmas brunch. He held her hand as they strolled along the water's edge.

They saw Tally, Julie, and Susan sitting on the beach, laughing, and called out a greeting to them as they passed. They headed a bit farther down the beach, then stopped, watching the waves roll into shore.

A breeze blew her hair back, and the foam from the waves lapped at her feet. "This has been the best day." She smiled up at Wade.

"It has. I think we should make a wish. You know, it's not just a legend. When you toss a shell into the sea at Lighthouse Point, your wish does come true."

"Do you think the wishes really come true?" She eyed him skeptically.

"I do. I firmly believe it." He nodded.

They both reached down, and the perfect shell called to her, so she picked it up, waiting for Wade to find one. Then they stood side by side. She closed her eyes, made a wish, opened her eyes, and tossed the shell into the water. His shell plopped into the water beside hers, sinking into the depths of the sea.

"What did you wish?" She turned and looked at him.

"I didn't make a wish. I said thanks for already giving me my wish."

She frowned. "I don't understand."

"I made a wish at Lighthouse Point right after you and your Mom left. I wished that you'd come back." He swept her hair back and cupped her face in his hands. "And I got my wish. I just didn't know it would take so long." His eyes shone in an intense burning blue.

Her breath whisked away. She steadied herself by holding onto his arms.

"What did you wish, Molls?"

She stared at him, trying to think. "Oh, it's probably silly. But I wished my parents could… you know… get together. That's crazy, isn't it?"

"Is it? Everything is possible when you make a wish at Lighthouse Point."

"But you should make a *new* wish." She nodded at him. "Pick a shell."

"Okay, okay." He leaned over and picked up a shell rippled with specks of light purple. He paused for a moment, then tossed it out into the water.

"What did you wish for now?" She looked up and his face turned serious.

"I wished you never had to leave," he whispered.

"I've been thinking about that. I think… I think I don't want to leave."

"You don't?" A wide grin spread across his face.

"No, I don't. I love it here. I love the island, the cottage, the people."

"You love the people?" His eyes locked with hers. "What people?"

A smile teased at the corner of her lips. "Some of my neighbors. I'm especially fond of one of them."

"The handsome dude who lives next door?"

"That very same one."

"That's very lucky for you," he said with a mock-serious expression. "Because that neighbor is very fond of you. In fact…"

She held her breath, waiting. Wanting. Needing to hear him say the words.

"In fact, I love you, Molly Croft."

Her heart soared, and she reached out and touched his cheek. "That's very good to hear because I'd hate to think I was the only one who loved someone in this relationship."

"Okay, that was kind of twisted… but did you just say you loved me?" He grinned, his eyes shining with emotion.

"Yes, I love you, Wade. I do. You make me happy. I can't imagine my life without you in it."

He laughed and swooped her up in his arms, twirling her around in a circle before putting her down. "But there's still one thing."

"What's that?" She frowned.

"There's that kiss I've been wanting."

She held her breath, waiting again, wanting again. He lowered his lips to hers and finally, finally, after all this time, he kissed her. She wrapped her arms around him, pulling him closer, feeling connected. She was home. Right here. In his arms.

He deepened their kiss and soon the world drifted away and she didn't know where she ended and he began.

They finally pulled apart, but he held onto her hands, grinning. "Looks like I was right."

"Right about what?"

"That wishes come true at Lighthouse Point. You're staying."

"I am staying. Staying forever. Right here. With you." She leaned against his broad chest, feeling his heart beat in rhythm with hers.

EPILOGUE

Next Year. Christmas Morning.

Molly stood at Wade's side after all the commotion of Christmas morning died down. Brunch eaten. Gifts exchanged. His parents sat on the couch, chatting with her parents.

She looked up at Wade and nodded. "Go ahead."

Wade cleared his throat. "So... Molls and I have a little announcement."

Their parents looked up at him expectantly.

Wade broke into a wide grin and pulled her close to his side. "We're engaged."

She slipped the ring out of her pocket where she'd hidden it for the morning and placed it back on her finger.

Her mother jumped up, rushed over, and looked at the ring. "It's beautiful, honey. I'm so happy for you."

Her father and Wade's parents came over and congratulated them. She stood by Wade's side, beaming as happiness swept through her.

"Well, if this is announcement time, I have one, too," her mother said, her eyes shining.

"What's that?" She eyed her mother, who looked particularly happy.

"Your mother and I are getting married." Her father threaded his arm around her mom's waist, beaming.

"Really?" She hugged her father, then popped over and caught herself before she hugged her mother, too.

Her mother stretched out her arms, and Molly walked into them, hugging her tightly. "Mom, I'm so happy for you."

"Me, too, Molly. I'm happy. More than I've ever been. It's taken us years to circle back to this point, but we made it. And I have to thank you for bringing us together."

"It wasn't really me. It was Shannon. She kept pushing for the truth to be out. She kept looking for Dad." Molly lifted her glass. "To Shannon."

"To Shannon, for always knowing what was the right thing to do." Her mother raised her glass.

"To Christmas on Belle Island with all of us and many more to come," Wade said as he looked down at her, smiling the special smile he had just for her. The one that warmed her heart and filled her with happiness.

Molly swore she could feel Shannon looking down on them. Smiling. Thinking that she'd finally made everything right.

And everything *was* right in her world.

I hope you enjoyed this holiday story set at Lighthouse Point. If you haven't read the whole Lighthouse Point series, you can start with book one, Wish Upon a Shell.

The Charming Inn series, a spin-off series

of Lighthouse Point, is available now. More of your favorite characters and places and three new best friends, Sara, Robin, and Charlotte. It starts with One Simple Wish - Book One.

Thanks for reading my stories. I truly appreciate each and every one of my readers. Happy reading.

ALSO BY KAY CORRELL

COMFORT CROSSING ~ THE SERIES

The Shop on Main - Book One

The Memory Box - Book Two

The Christmas Cottage - A Holiday Novella (Book 2.5)

The Letter - Book Three

The Christmas Scarf - A Holiday Novella (Book 3.5)

The Magnolia Cafe - Book Four

The Unexpected Wedding - Book Five

The Wedding in the Grove (crossover short story between series - Josephine and Paul from The Letter.)

LIGHTHOUSE POINT ~ THE SERIES

Wish Upon a Shell - Book One

Wedding on the Beach - Book Two

Love at the Lighthouse - Book Three

Cottage near the Point - Book Four

Return to the Island - Book Five

Bungalow by the Bay - Book Six

Christmas Comes to Lighthouse Point - Book Seven

CHARMING INN ~ Return to Lighthouse Point

One Simple Wish - Book One

Two of a Kind - Book Two

Three Little Things - Book Three

Four Short Weeks - Book Four

Five Years or So - Book Five

Six Hours Away - Book Six

Charming Christmas - Book Seven

SWEET RIVER ~ THE SERIES

A Dream to Believe in - Book One

A Memory to Cherish - Book Two

A Song to Remember - Book Three

A Time to Forgive - Book Four

A Summer of Secrets - Book Five

A Moment in the Moonlight - Book Six

MOONBEAM BAY ~ THE SERIES

The Parker Women - Book One

The Parker Cafe - Book Two

A Heather Parker Original - Book Three

The Parker Family Secret - Book Four

Grace Parker's Peach Pie - Book Five

The Perks of Being a Parker - Book Six

BLUE HERON COTTAGES ~ THE SERIES

Memories of the Beach - Book One

Walks along the Shore - Book Two

Bookshop by the Bay - Book Three

Plus more to come!

WIND CHIME BEACH ~ A stand-alone novel

INDIGO BAY ~ Save by getting Kay's complete collection of stories previously published separately in the multi-author Indigo Bay series. The three stories are all interconnected.

Sweet Days by the Bay - the collection

ABOUT THE AUTHOR

Kay Correll is a USA Today bestselling author of sweet, heartwarming stories that are a cross between women's fiction and contemporary romance. She is known for her charming small towns, quirky townsfolk, and the enduring strong friendships between the women in her books.

Kay splits her time between the Southwest coast of Florida and the Midwest of the U.S. and can often be found out and about with her camera, taking a myriad of photographs, often incorporating them into her book covers. When not lost in her writing or photography, she can be found spending time with her ever-supportive husband, knitting, or playing with her puppies - a cavalier who is too cute for his own good and a naughty but adorable Australian shepherd. Their five boys are all grown now and while she misses the rowdy boy-noise chaos, she is thoroughly enjoying her empty nest years.

Learn more about Kay and her books at kaycorrell.com

While you're there, sign up for her newsletter to hear about new releases, sales, and giveaways.

WHERE TO FIND ME:
kaycorrell.com
authorcontact@kaycorrell.com

Join my Facebook Reader Group. We have lots of fun and you'll hear about sales and new releases first!
www.facebook.com/groups/KayCorrell/

I love to hear from my readers. Feel free to contact me at authorcontact@kaycorrell.com

f facebook.com/KayCorrellAuthor
instagram.com/kaycorrell
pinterest.com/kaycorrellauthor
a amazon.com/author/kaycorrell
BB bookbub.com/authors/kay-correll

Made in the USA
Coppell, TX
27 June 2024

34013779R00163